TIME FOR PEACE

BOOK #7 IN THE MAMA B SERIES

MICHELLE STIMPSON

DEDICATION

For my grandmother, the Mama B in my life.

ACKNOWLEDGMENTS

Thank You, Lord, for the words to share with my sisters and brothers in Christ. I'm honored to minister through writing. I'm honored to share the good news through art, and I give You all the praise for this!

Thank you to the fans and readers who encourage me so much along this journey. It's been a long time since we've heard from Mama B. I'm thankful for your all letting me know how much this character (especially) and my books (in general) bless you. I'm humbled and glad to be a part of your life in Him.

Kellie Gilbert, Lynne Gentry, CaSandra McLaughlin, and Vanessa Miller, you always give me good ideas and encourage me as fellow writers and as sisters in the Lord. Thanks for your advice on this book!

Thanks to my advance readers to helping spread the news. I'm grateful for you!

Thanks, Karen McCollum Rodgers, for your editing eye.

Finally, to my family – I pray that, as I grow in Him, I will be a bit of a 'Mama B' to you. I'm blessed to have you all.

BEFORE YOU START READING...

Let me say THANK YOU so much for purchasing this book! I pray it will be an entertaining, encouraging read for you. Click below if you'd like to join my email list and receive notice of new books and contests and keep in touch, visit the link: http://bit.ly/JoinMStimpsonList.

Again, many thanks!!!

Michelle Stimpson

ALSO BY MICHELLE STIMPSON

Deacon Brown's Daughters - Stanley Brown's got a lot of cleaning up to do if he wants to become a deacon...and it starts with his children.

War Room Strategies – A step-by-step guide to developing effectual prayers for God's Glory

Stuck on You - Braxton Stoneworth and Tiffany Warren were just friends in college...until one spring night when the love bug bit. But Braxton threw it all away to join his fraternity. Will Tiffany forgive him ten years later?

Boaz Brown – When LaShondra Smith prayed for the right man, she forgot to specify his race. Can she see past the wrapping paper to receive the gift?

1

Lord knows I don't like gettin' no phone calls after ten o'clock at night. That's why I turn off my ringer on my iPhone. Anybody who really needs me gotta call on the house phone, which is exactly what happened one warm summer night not too long after me and Frank had settled into bed.

I reached over to the nightstand to answer. "Hello?"

"Beatrice! This house is haunted!" Ida Mae always had a penchant for exaggeration, otherwise known as lying.

"Calm down. What's going on?" I sat up in bed and switched on the lamp.

Frank turned toward me, obviously listening in on the conversation.

Ida Mae continued, "I heard a loud groaning

sound, then swoosh! Sounded like the water flowing back into the orange sea right after Abraham and them crossed!"

Never mind it was Moses who *parted* the *Red* Sea, not Abraham. And never mind the fact Ida Mae probably ain't never even read that chapter in the Bible—she just goin' off a Hollywood movie.

"So I went down the hallway to the sound; there was all this water gushing out of the toilet. First it was muddy. Then it was white, like it's coming straight from the city line."

Frank whispered, "Ask her did she turn off the supply?"

I repeated his question to her.

"Yeah. It took me a while, with my arthritis and all. I hope I didn't hurt myself tryin' to save *your* house. But yeah, I got it turned off. Now the bathroom's a mess. I've been trying to keep the water in this area, but I can't stop it from going all down the hallway. I need some more hands over here!"

I wasn't sure how much help my untrained hands would be, but I hopped out of bed anyway.

Frank followed suit.

"We're on our way," I assured Ida Mae.

FRANK DIDN'T SAY much on the way over to my previous home. I knew he was thinking about something. When I asked him what was on his mind, he said, "We can talk about it later. One thing at a time."

I sent my oldest boy, Son, a text message to let him know something had gone wrong with the plumbing in the house. Son calls himself the landlord over my old property, but he really ain't doin' nothing more than paying the taxes on the house every year since I rented it out to Ida Mae, my deceased first husband's sister. I'm not even sure if Albert would have wanted Ida Mae staying there, but if the truth be told, she was doing me a favor. I needed a tenant, she needed a place to stay. You know how the saying goes: Better the devil you know than the devil you don't.

Lord, forgive me. Ida Mae ain't really the devil. She just *Ida Mae* and we ain't never been the best of friends. Some people you just got to learn to tolerate in order to keep peace until Jesus come back.

I hope He come back soon.

Anyhow, we made it to the house in Peasner, TX in twenty minutes since there was no traffic at that time of night. Out of respect for Ida Mae, I rang the doorbell and we waited for her to answer even though I already had the key. It had taken me a while, but I was finally to the point where I recognized that even though this was the house my first husband had built and we'd raised our family in, I didn't live there anymore. I had a new life with my second husband, Frank. I lived in a different house in a different city. I still had a lot of memories at the old house, but I was making plenty new ones with Frank in our neighborhood.

Ida Mae was taking her sweet time opening the door. I pressed the doorbell several more times. Still no answer. "What's wrong with her?" I fussed Frank. "She tryin' to melt us like chocolate out here?" Despite the time of night, it was still pretty warm. That's how the summer is in Texas.

Frank stole a kiss from my cheek. "You sure are sweet to me, with your chocolate brown skin."

The kissed spot on my face made me giggle. Frank does that to me sometimes.

He reached past me and rang the doorbell again. Then he squeezed in closer to the door and rang it again, this time with his ear almost on the wood. "B, I don't hear the chime on the other side. Is the doorbell working?"

This time we both listened carefully as he pressed again.

"I'll be. I think you're onto something, Frank."

We both started beating on the door, so Ida Mae could hear us.

She came within a matter of seconds that time and let us inside. Her head was tied in a red, satin scarf. She was dressed in a blue cotton pajama set that was slightly darker at the bottom, I assumed from the water she had encountered.

"Ida Mae, how long the doorbell been broke?" I asked.

She rolled her eyes. "I don't know. A week or two, I guess."

"Well, you got to tell us when stuff ain't workin'. Elsewise, how we gonna know to fix it?" I fussed as I followed her down the main hallway to the bathroom.

"If I called you for every little knob coming off and every little tile peeling up, I'd have to talk to you all day, and you know I'm not trying to do that."

The feeling was mutual. But this was business. "Well, you could at least let Son know."

I heard the sloshing sound beneath my feet and gasped at the small flood under my shoes. "This is a mess!"

"I told you," Ida Mae agreed.

Frank forged ahead of us into the bathroom. Ida Mae and I remained in the hall. Though I wasn't the one inspecting the situation, it was clear that, despite the towels spread across the hallway carpet, there was still enough standing water to do damage to the walls if left overnight.

A few minutes later, Frank came out of the bathroom. "We're going to have to get somebody out here now. Can't leave it like this while we're gone out of town." He whipped out his cell phone and headed back toward the kitchen.

Ida Mae stood with her hands on her hips. "I can't

use this bathroom anymore." She yanked her head toward the dysfunctional room.

"I see." I looked around and sighed.

"That means this space is off limits to me."

I nodded. "Agreed. But you've got a private bathroom where you sleep."

"But I can't use *this* one," she reiterated.

I crossed my arms. "What you tryin' to say, Ida Mae?"

Her neck slid to the side. "I'm saying I want a reduction on my rent. Until you all get this fixed. And a bunch of other stuff around here, too."

Now, mind you, she was already paying far less rent than what I woulda charged anybody else. Plus, I hadn't raised the rent the whole time she had been staying there. Going on four years. Plus, she had been late a time or two paying the bill and we'd never charged her any late fees. But now that she was down to one bathroom, she wanna claim her rights.

Two can play at that game. "Well now, since you didn't inform us of the other so-called problems before today, you can't rightly blame us for them not being fixed in a timely manner."

"Still," she insisted with a haughty expression, "the entire square footage of the house is not available to me. I've lost a full night of sleep in all this. And my wrist is hurtin' from turnin' off the water. My rent should be reduced accordingly." She held her arm to her chest like somebody in need of an arm sling.

You know what? It was too late and too hot to be arguing with this woman. "Fine. How about fifty dollars off?"

"A hundred."

"Seventy."

"Eighty," she countered.

"Seventy-five and that's my final offer."

"Fine. But if my brother was living, he wouldn't have charged me a red cent until this house was in tip-top condition. Albert took *pride* in his belongings."

I didn't have the heart to tell her that if my ex-husband were still living, I'd still be living in this house and she wouldn't hardly be able to set foot inside, let alone spend a night.

I cleared my throat. "Seventy-five off. Period. And don't be late next month or I'll have to enforce the fee."

She huffed. "You gon' play tit for tat with me now?"

"You started it," I reminded her. "Now, me and Frank will take the clean-up from here. You can go on back to bed. We'll lock up on the way out."

Ida Mae turned sharply, sloshed down the hall-way, and slammed the door to the master bedroom.

I joined Frank in the kitchen. By then, he'd already summoned help. The plumbers were on their way, all too eager to charge after-hours rates to do the work.

While we waited, I poured us two glasses of iced tea. Ida Mae would probably fuss about us using her groceries, but she would just have to get over it. I was tired of fooling with her. I was tired, period. It was going on eleven o'clock by then. Me and Frank had to get up and out the next day for a flight to a wedding.

I handed Frank his glass and sat at the kitchen table with him.

"You want to tell me what's on your mind?" I asked in the still silence of the kitchen.

He took a cautious swallow. Looked up at the ceiling. Down at the floors. Sideways at the cabinets.

I followed his eyes, catching glimpses of water marks, worn spots, and crooked hinges.

"B," Frank said softly, "that situation in the bathroom looks serious. We're not getting any younger. Neither is this house. I think it may be time to sell."

2

I didn't say anything one way or the other when Frank said what he said about the house. My first thought was that it wasn't none of Frank's business what I decided to do with the house my first husband left me.

But then when we got back home and Frank climbed back in the bed two hours later, tired and worn, I realized he *did* have a dog in this fight. Whatever happened to that house concerned me. And whatever concerned me concerned him. I needed to think like a couple.

Of course, that would be easier if there were no kids involved. My four—Son, Debra Kay, Cassandra, and Otha—would have something to say. They all had memories and emotions tied to the house. Well, maybe not Otha since he's my busy child, but I imagined the rest of them might feel some kind of way.

When me and Frank got up the next morning, I made sure to fix him a good breakfast. Made him a waffle, some eggs with cheese, and poured him a nice, tall glass of orange juice. He deserved it.

I only had toast and tea. Had too much on my mind to eat.

"You awfully quiet this morning," Frank said, taking a seat across from me at the table. Since school was out for the summer break and Frank had taken off time for the trip, this was one of our rare lazy mornings together. My little neighbor friend, Jeffrey, wouldn't be coming over for breakfast and Frank wasn't rushing off to work. The Lord knows how to time stuff just right. Me and Frank needed some time to discuss his suggestion, albeit unsolicited.

I took a sip of tea. "Been thinkin' about what you said last night. About the house."

"I figured such." He chewed slowly. Swallowed. "And?"

"I don't know," I admitted. "I had a lot of good times in that house. Son's gonna fight me till the bitter end about it."

"There's no reason why he can't buy the house and keep it in the family," Frank said.

"What if I just transferred the deed?"

Frank shrugged. "Not a good *business* deal, but it's

up to you. My whole point is I don't want us to be burdened with the responsibility of keeping up two households at our age."

Now, everything Frank said made perfect sense in a perfect world. But I know a thing or two about estates and wills and how greed come creeping around after people die. Things can get real *im*perfect real quick. I had to go there. "And what about *this* house? Suppose we sell my house, and then you pass before me. I don't want to be fighting your family to keep a roof over my head. So long as I got my own house paid for outright, I'll never have to worry about a place to stay."

Frank tilted his head in agreement. "I'll have a talk with my family and my attorney. Make sure we get it all taken care of. I don't ever want you to worry about being taken care of, B. I want to look out for you whether I'm here or not." He patted my hand gently.

I took his fingers and squeezed them. God sure did put some good, solid men into my life. The kind of men that made vows and took pride in providing for their wives and families. Might not have had everything we wanted, but we always had what we needed. And all the glory goes to Him because He's the one that gave them the strength and wherewithal to keep those promises.

Thank You, Lord.

"Well, I might as well start with Son." I sighed.

Frank grabbed my other hand and said a prayer, asking the Lord to lead us and guide us to the best decision. He spoke peace over both of our families and thanked the Lord in advance for working out everything for our good because we love Him.

"Amen," I agreed at the end of Frank's prayer.

"I'm going to run to the hospital real quick and tie up a few loose ends before we leave."

"Now, Frank, don't *you* get tied up. We need to leave for the airport no later than ten."

"I hear you, woman," he teased. Frank smacked my lips with his. "Since we gon' be gone for a week, I know you got a thousand bags. Have 'em ready to load up when I get back."

"For your information, I do *not* have a thousand bags," I insisted.

"All right. Have all nine hundred and ninety-nine right there." He pointed at the door to the garage.

"Mmm hmmm," I mumbled and smiled.

AFTER FRANK LEFT, I didn't have a whole lot of time to finish my last minute packing and get myself together. And with us being up so late at the old house, I didn't get my usual rest. Still, I knew talkin' to Son would require some extra spiritual reinforcement because he could be just as stubborn as his father.

I happened to be readin' a devotional by Andrew

Murray. He dead and gone, but the truth he wrote about Jesus is still alive and well. Mr. Murray was writin' about abiding in Christ. How He lives in us and we live in Him, branch to vine. Even more than that, he made reference to some Scriptures and I promise you, chile, when I looked 'em up it was like I had never seen them before in my entire life! I tell you, it feels like Christmas day when I come across a Word and get a whole new level of understandin' about life with the Lord! I believe it's near 'bout impossible to grow old in Jesus with the Word renewin' your mind fresh every day.

That day wasn't no different. One of Mr. Murray's paragraphs took me to Galatians 4:6. "And because ye are sons, God hath sent forth the Spirit of his Son into your hearts, crying, Abba, Father." Now, I know I done studied the book of Galatians before and I'm sure I've read that Scripture before. But when I read that part about the Spirit of his Son in my heart—this seventy-five-year-old heart that's done seen plenty of good and bad—to think His actual Spirit is in me and with me all the time...whew! I couldn't take it. I just sat there and wept. Then I flipped over to Romans 5:5 where it says God has also poured His love into our hearts. He sure do a lot of pourin'! I'm so glad to stand still and receive.

After I got myself recomposed, I wrote a little something in my journal thanking the Lord for His ways. I wrote Him about Son and the house and Frank and how I was getting kind of scared because what if I ended up without a place to stay behind all this? And all of a sudden this question popped in my mind: *On what day in your life were you takin' care of you, Beatrice?* I put my pen down. Crossed my arms.

God's got a way of speakin' a word even when He's askin' a question. In all my days, I might have felt like He wasn't there, but when I got far enough away to see things in hindsight—and I got a lotta decades to look back over now—He's always provided some kind of way.

I nodded. Then I started laughing because I could almost feel Him laughing in me. "Abba, Father, You right. And You really something special, you know that?" Anybody peepin' in my window probably would have thought I was crazy, sitting there laughing and talking to my invisible Daddy, but me and God... we do that sometimes.

I forced myself to get this initial call to Son out of the way. Didn't want it weighing heavy on my mind all through the trip, trying to bring fear back into my mind. Sometimes you just need to go ahead and cut the enemy off at the pass, you know?

I pressed the call icon on my phone next to Son's name. That time of morning, I knew he'd be driving to work.

When he answered, the sound of a horn blaring

followed by him fussing at somebody for cutting him off gave me pause. "Son?"

"Momma, these people on the highway are going to make me lose my mind!"

"Don't speak those words over yourself, Son. Calm down, now, I gotta talk to you."

He huffed and puffed a little more. Then he finally asked, "What is it, Momma?"

"Well, first of all, you didn't bother to call me back last night about the water predicament at the house."

"I just saw the text this morning, and I was running late, so I didn't get to answer you."

"How you gon' call yourself the landlord and I'm the one fixin' all the problems?"

A loud honk came through the phone again. This time, Son used a cussword against someone on the road.

"Son!" Now, I knew my oldest child was no stranger to profanity, but I taught all my kids not to disrespect elders in word or deed.

"Momma, I'm sorry. This commute is killing me both to and from work."

"If this new job is causing you this much stress every day, you need to quit," I told him. "I know good and well it must take you an hour to get your mind right once you clock in."

"I'm on salary. I don't clock in," he corrected me.

"Well, you 'bout to clock *out* if you keep raisin' your blood pressure like this every morning."

I loaded the breakfast dishes into the dishwasher, popped in a square of detergent, and started the machine.

"I'm almost at work now. What do you need?"

"I need to talk to you about the house, Son. Me and Frank been thinkin'. Maybe it's time to—"

"Don't tell me you're about to say sell." Son beat me to the punch.

"You gon' let me talk?"

"Not if you're about to say what I think you're going to say."

"I'm gonna say it anyway. Me and Frank gettin' long in the tooth. And I hate to say it, but you ain't no reliable landlord. Now, if you or one of the other kids want to buy the house, that's perfectly fine. We can keep it in the family." I tried to temper the news the same way Frank gave it to me.

Son's end was silent.

"You there?"

"Yes. I knew it would come to this. I knew Frank would eventually do this."

I felt my neck jerk back. "Do what?"

"Try to come in and take over."

"Take over *what*?"

"Everything. You. The house."

I needed somebody to come in and pick my chin up off the floor. "Run that by me again."

"Frank has brainwashed you into selling the house."

My whole body started feeling jittery 'cause can't nobody talk bad about my husband except me, and even I don't do it. These words coming out of Son's mouth hit me so hard in such a soft spot, I didn't have no doubt they was comin' straight from the enemy. No tellin' how much he'd been whispering to my oldest about me and Frank, and Son ain't got the spiritual wisdom to spot the devil's foolishment. Now, Son ought to be able to discern since he fifty-something in human years, but I reckon he couldn't have been no more than fifteen in spirit-years in order to believe that batch of lies.

"Albert Jackson Junior, you are out of line."

"I can't talk about this right now. I gotta go." Son ended the call without so much as a good-bye.

I ain't gon' sit here and lie; Son really hurt my feelings. I knew he wasn't gung-ho about the idea of me marryin' Frank, seeing as I was in my seventies. But it ain't like Frank was some broke rascal tryin' to get some stability from me. Frank was still a practicing doctor with plenty of his own money when we married. All our kids were grown and on their own, doing fine. Wasn't nobody to mooch off of nobody nowhere in our arrangements. If anything, I'm the one always bringin' the stray, moochin'-folk home with me, not Frank.

Wasn't nothin' for me to do but get back in the prayer closet 'cause sticky situations like this be itchin' to explode if they ain't handled prayerfully.

3

Frank was a little put out with me 'cause I wasn't quite ready when he got home at 9:45. My husband don't like to be late for nothin'. I tried to tell him we wasn't officially late because we did close the door to the house at 10:00 a.m. and he did crank up the car and put it in reverse at 10:01 a.m.

"But B, you fussed plenty at me before I left. Then when I got home, you were still curling your hair."

Now, I know I wasn't guilty of no wrong-doing, technically speaking, since we did leave the house on time. But sometimes you got to decide it's better to have peace than to be right.

"Honey, I'm sorry." I ran my hand across the back of his head. "I should have been ready sooner." It was the truth. And I *would* have been ready sooner if it hadn't been for the way Son acted, which put me back in the prayer closet for another fifteen minutes, so I could get my mind settled and speak some constructive words into the situation before I left 'cause them words be workin' even when we involved in something altogether different.

"You forgive me?" I batted my lashes.

Frank glanced at me. "You know I do."

"Thank you kindly."

The smirk on his face let me know the situation was over and done with. We could enjoy each other on this trip to Miami Beach. Beaches, cool breezes, beautiful scenery, and love in the air. His colleague, Dr. Gary Westhouse, was getting remarried after being divorced for three years. I wasn't one to be all in people's business, but this man's business was in the news for a while there because his wife had made the divorce very public. People love a good scandal. I don't know how much she got paid for airing all their dirty laundry, but I hope it was a pretty penny for all she was posting and texting and sharing with the news media in our town.

Like I said, I wasn't following the stories, but I gathered enough to know she was accusing him of cheating and he was accusing her of the same. Basically it was a mess.

I came in on the tail end of things with Gary and his first wife, seeing as me and Frank hadn't been married very long. I don't really socialize with Frank's doctor friends outside of the Christmas parties and fundraisers and such. I really didn't even know Gary was engaged, but when Frank said Gary had asked him to be in the wedding and we'd get an all-expense-paid week on the beach, I didn't ask no questions. All I did was make some phone calls to get my calendar in order. I called my friend, Libbie, and let her know I wouldn't be at the shelter for a week. Then I called my best friend, Ophelia, and told her I wouldn't be at the exercise class or at the church because I was headed for sand and sun.

"Oooh, B! That's so romantic!" she exclaimed. "Me and Pastor gon' have to make our way out there some-time soon!"

Seem like every time she said 'Pastor,' I still had to remind myself that she had married our pastor a few years earlier.

My last call was to Debra Kay, my oldest daughter. Once I told her, that was like telling the rest of the family, Son included. Debra Kay encouraged me to have a good time and bring her something back. I assured her I would.

And now we were on our way to Miami Beach. Frank and I were the first ones to arrive at the airport. Now, see, the old me—when I was first married to Albert and didn't know how to let stuff go—would have told my husband that he had made a fuss about me not being ready for no reason after all. But like I said earlier, the situation was over. You can't keep bringin' up stuff once you done agreed to settle it.

Instead, I sat down next to Frank and tilted my straw hat back a little and started reading a short mystery book on my iPhone. Reading fiction books is something I've always enjoyed. I just don't get much time to do it until I'm on vacation or something.

I was settling into the characters when I heard Dr. Westhouse call Frank's name. Frank and I stood up to greet him.

"Thanks again, Buddy," Gary said, giving my husband a hug. "B, always a pleasure to see you as well."

"Glad to join in your joy, Dr. Westhouse," I said.

"Please. Call me Gary," he said. "We're family this weekend."

He gave me a proper A-frame hug, which gave me a chance to look at the disinterested young lady behind him who was busy thumbing away on her phone screen. I figured she was his daughter or something, though Frank had told me most of Gary's family actually lived in southern Florida and would simply drive to the wedding.

Gary turned to the side and held out his arm toward the young lady. "Frank, B, this is my fiancée, Kennedy."

I blinked. Twice. *Really?*

The girl flipped her brownish-red hair back across

her shoulder. She looked up at us like she was graciously giving us the attention we didn't deserve. "Hello. Thanks for coming." I guess she was trying her best to put on a smile, but it wasn't working.

Frank shook Kennedy's hand as though there was no problem at all. "Kennedy. So good to meet you. Gary talks about you all the time. You're just as beautiful as he described."

With that compliment, a more genuine smile covered Kennedy's face. "Awww...how sweet!" She pecked Gary on the cheek.

"B has never been to Florida. We'll have to show her a wonderful time," Frank added.

"We sure will." Kennedy and I shook hands. "It's a beautiful state. Gary and I got engaged there."

"Oh, really. How long y'all been engaged?" To tell the truth, in my mind I was tryin' to figure out if this was the little lady who had done stole him from his wife.

Kennedy thrust her left hand forward for me to see the large diamond plopped on her ring finger as though I'd asked her to show me proof of their engagement.

I wasn't about to give her no compliments until she answered my question. "Oh, good. You have a ring. And how long y'all been together?"

She lowered her hand. "A little over a year."

"Well, that's...that's a year!" I nodded at both

Kennedy and Gary.

Frank put an arm around my waist. "We're going to head to the restroom. You'll watch our bags for us?"

"Certainly," Gary said.

Frank practically dragged me away and out of sight. We ducked into a coffee shop a few gates down.

"B. Stop it."

"Stop what?"

"Judging them based on their age difference."

I closed my lips. Thought about what to say for a second. Wasn't no use in me denying it because I was doing exactly what he accused me of. It's just so odd, seeing these older men trade in their first or even second wives for a newer model. It ain't right. And I got a hard time actin' like everything is okay when it's not.

"Frank, you know me. You should have told me before we got here that he was marryin' somebody half his age."

"What difference does it make? We're still going to the beach. We're still going to have a wonderful time, and two people are still getting married."

"Yes, but—"

"But they don't look like you want them to. Right?"

"That's not what I'm saying."

Frank crossed his arms. "Then what *are* you saying?"

"I'm saying this is a surprise to me."

"Well, surprise, surprise, surprise," he imitated Gomer Pyle. "Now, I'mma need you to get over this and enjoy yourself 'cause I don't want to see you mopin' around about something you really don't even know about except for what you see on the outside."

I looked around at the patrons in the coffee shop. Most had cell phones in one hand, cups in the other. Oblivious to their surroundings.

"Did you see how she was on her cell phone?"

He shrugged. "That's what the young folk do."

"I know! What Dr. Westhouse got in common with her? He gotta be at least fifty-five and she *might* be thirty! What they gon' do every evening—him sit up and watch the news while she scrollin' through that Snap-flat stuff?"

Frank laughed. "First of all, it's Snap*chat*. Second, it wasn't but five minutes ago, you were sitting next to me reading a book *on your phone.*"

"There's a difference between a book and a text message," I sassed.

"Was your face buried in a phone or not?"

I rolled my eyes downward. He had me. "I suppose."

"Then live and let live, B. Now, are you going to fuss and complain the whole time we're here? 'Cause if you are, we might as well stay home."

I gasped. "Are you serious?"

"Yes. I don't want to have to run interference for

you on this trip. Now, leave all that critical stuff here in Texas. You can pick it up when you get back if you want to, but that just means I'll pray over you and God'll break it. We can do this the easy way or the hard way, B."

Me and Frank don't always see eye-to-eye on how to deal with folks. One minute I want to open up our house to everyone in need and he don't. The next minute he lettin' somebody drink a beer in the house and I'm 'bout ready to throw them out. We both love the Lord, but we still got our differences and we still got a ways to go to look just like Jesus.

I took a deep breath. "Okay, Frank. I've decided to have a good attitude."

He kissed my cheek. "I knew you would 'cause Jesus had a good attitude everywhere He went."

I tell you one thing, sometimes I think the Holy Spirit be goin' back and tellin' Frank what He and I discuss in private. But I supposed that's how He works when a couple is dedicated to lovin' Him and lovin' each other, too.

Me and Frank rejoined Kennedy and Gary at our gate. By then, two other couples and some more young people had joined us. Somehow, having the other people around helped me to get over myself. So long as the bride and groom were happy, I guessed I could be, too. Who am I to put asunder what God has joined together...assumin' He had done the joinin'.

4

———

Whatever attitude the enemy might have thought he was going to brew up in me got sidetracked as we made it to Miami Beach. The breeze, the smell of the ocean and the picture-book hotel we were staying at swept all my troubles away. The sand and the sun, the smell of the water, the fresh air. I tell you, it was straight from a postcard and a pleasant dream.

This place reminded me of that old TV show, Fantasy Island. Just beautiful and easy-going. Plenty of folk our age was there, too, which always puts me at ease. You know, I don't have no problem with the younger generation in general, but they always tryin' to rush thangs. They tryin' to scroll through life like it's something to be glimpsed on a screen rather than lived in reality. This place right here, though, would make anybody put their cell phone down and look at what God Himself had created.

Even Kennedy and her crew got wide-eyed when we arrived at our grounds for the week. I took hold of Frank's free hand and squeezed it. He looked down at me. I motioned for him to bend down. When he did, I kissed him.

He smiled. "What was that for?"

"For bringin' me here. This is mighty pretty, Frank. Mighty pretty."

"Ain't no prettier than what you see in the mirror every day." He winked at me.

I giggled and slapped his arm. "You too much, Romeo."

Out the corner of my eye, I seen Kennedy and two of her friends starin' at me and Frank. One of them had her finger in her mouth like she was tryin' to make herself throw up, making fun of me and my husband. Soon as I snapped my head toward them, all three of them quickly turned away, laughing to themselves. That confirmed my suspicion 'cause ain't hardly no time three people make the exact same move at the exact same moment 'less they all in on something.

There's one thing about gettin' old I don't like: People seem to think you can't hear or see or think straight. Some people my age can't, but a lot of us still can. We know more than folk give us credit for, we just wise enough not to tell it all.

It's annoying sometimes. I wasn't about to let nothing and no one stand in the way of me enjoying my time at the beach, though. Not even the bride and her little clan.

When Dr. Westhouse finished checking us all into the hotel, he huddled us up and gave us our keys.

The wedding coordinator, a middle-aged woman with a strong tan named Larissa, introduced herself and gave us directions for what to do next. "Get settled into your rooms. You'll find the week's itinerary on your nightstands, starting with dinner this evening at LaPerazza, which is the restaurant here on the main floor. We'll eat at six. Be sure your clocks are set to Eastern time."

I changed my wristwatch accordingly.

"Are there any questions?" Larissa asked.

One of the younger girls who wasn't so tied to Kennedy's hip raised her hand. "What kind of cuisine do they serve at La Perazza?"

"*Free* cuisine," Kennedy answered instead of Larissa. "Just be grateful you're even here, Whitney." She rolled her eyes, shook her head, and huffed, dismissing the girl's question altogether.

Well, it's been a long time since I heard something that rude up close and personal. Not since the visiting minister, Falanda, came and got herself all tied up with the city of Peasner police when she came to visit my old church, Mt. Zion. That was a mess, and I could see whatever problems Whitney and Kennedy had was nasty, too.

"I'm asking because of my allergies," Whitney finally defended herself.

Larissa said, "La Perazza's is known for their Mexican cuisine, but they serve American classics, too. I'm sure you'll find something on the menu that won't give you trouble."

"Thanks. I appreciate *your* kindness, unlike some *other* people."

Thatta girl, Whitney!

"You're welcome," Larissa said, ignoring the way Kennedy was stabbing Whitney with her eyes. "Let's all line up near the concierge to be transported to our rooms."

About four of us at a time could get on the little golf carts. The grounds were so expansive, it would have taken us twenty minutes to walk to our quarters, not to mention the hassle of the luggage.

Me and Frank was in Room 3118 in a building named "Rockefeller" and I tell you, our room was fit for the Rockefeller family indeed. Gold columns, wine-colored draperies, and furniture fit for a king. This room was the kind of place them big old furniture stores put on the front of their catalogs: rugs, funny-shaped throw pillows with tassels, antique lamps. You name it, they put all the finishing touches on our room.

Now, me and my first husband, Albert, wasn't poor so it wasn't like I hadn't never stayed in a nice hotel. Albert was, however, thrifty. He paid a little extra, so we could have a hotel with doors inside the building, but that was about it.

I should have known Frank and his doctor friends was more apt to enjoy the finer things. Especially in our older age when we real clear about the fact tomorrow ain't promised. I imagine if Albert hadn't of died in his sixties, he might have come to the point where he'd put us up somewhere with these nice marble floors.

Them floors wasn't nothin' compared to the floors Albert was walkin' on in heaven, though, God rest his soul.

"This is so niiiiiice," I whispered to Frank for the tenth time.

"It is," he agreed. "Dr. Westhouse went all out."

"He sure did. We gotta be sure and thank him."

"Don't thank him. Thank Kennedy. She's the one who wanted an extravagant beach wedding and all these excursions. You see this?"

Frank handed me the paper Larissa had referred to. Dinner every night, a snorkeling adventure, jet skiing—both which I already knew I wasn't gonna do —a Karaoke Night, a barbeque night. The only day we had to ourselves was Thursday. There was also extra stuff on the agenda for the people in the wedding—spa day, photo shoots, hair and makeup times. "This girl done turned the wedding into a conference, almost."

Frank laughed. "Gary would have been content with a small ceremony at home. But this is her first marriage, so he gave in."

"Hmmm. Makes sense," I said. "Every girl has a dream about her wedding day."

"If you say so, B."

We had a few hours until it was time for us to eat, so I decided to take another shower. Being on a plane with all those strangers, sharing the same breathing air just makes my skin crawl.

Frank took over the television remote control and laid back on the bed while I performed my usual hotel cleaning. I pulled out the little canister of Lysol I'd packed and wiped off the handles and knobs, the light switches and the toilet seat. I took the remote from Frank for a second to sanitize it, too. He also had to stand while I gave the sheets a good germ-killing spray. Of course he scoffed, but he knew better than to try to stop a woman in the middle of her cleaning routine. Mind you, I'm not no kind of obsessive person when it comes to cleanliness. I got plenty of little areas of my own house I need to clean out, but

I'm okay with my germs. It's *other* people's germs I don't fool with.

Satisfied that I'd gotten rid of any leftover cooties, I then handled the business of washing up in the bathroom. I thought I heard my phone ringing in the middle of the shower, but then the sound stopped, so I wasn't sure if I was just hearing things.

When I finished dressing and came out the bathroom, I asked Frank about it.

"Yeah. Your phone rang," he confirmed.

"Who was it?"

Frank clicked through a few channels. Finally, he answered, "Son."

"Oh! What did he say?"

My husband still wasn't looking me in my eyes. "He gave me two estimates on the plumbing. Told me about something else going on in the house."

"Oh no!" I stomped toward the desk, where I thought I'd placed my phone. I didn't see the phone right away, so I started shuffling through my purse.

"I've got your phone, B. Turned it off."

"Whatever for?"

Frank sucked his teeth. "'Cause I've already handled the situation."

"I thought you said Son had estimates. He ain't made no final decisions yet."

"*I* made a final decision. I told him to handle it

however he deemed best," Frank said. "I also reminded him that we are on vacation."

Oh, Lord. Judging by the way my husband was still starin' hard at the television and by Son's harsh words that morning, I knew there had to be more to their talk than Frank was letting on. "Okaaay...and he said?"

"I'm not going to repeat the whole conversation. Suffice it to say the house will be taken care of. And Son will not be calling us anymore while we're in Miami Beach unless there is an emergency he can't tend to on his own."

"Frank. Look at me."

He raised an eyebrow, gave me a glance.

"Did you and Son have an argument?"

"No, 'cause I ain't gonna argue with Son."

I knew he was telling the truth. Frank don't hardly argue with nobody. He speak his peace and that's it; he ain't about to go round and round in circles with you.

"Well, was Son upset?"

"Yes."

I sighed and sat on the bed next to Frank. "Don't you think I should call him and smooth things out? I don't want him mad all week."

Frank mashed a button on the remote and the television went mute. He looked at me squarely. "B. You know I love you. And I love your family, too. But you must stop worrying about Son so much. If he chooses to be upset because I asked him to perform the landlord's duties we pay him for, that's on him."

"I don't want him to be upset, though. He's already stressed out about his job and—"

"When has Son *not* been stressed out and upset about something or another, B?"

Ooooh weeee! Frank be askin' questions almost as good as God do. I sat there and tried to remember when Son wasn't stressed and when he wasn't busy stressin' me out. If you want to know the truth, I couldn't think of too many times in this century when me and Son wasn't fussin' about Wanda or Nikki or his grandson, Cameron, or something about the house, or why Son wasn't going to church, or Frank, or Son's job...the list went on and on.

"You got a point. Me and Son do pick at each other a lot."

"That's because he loves you. And you love him. And y'all stick to your convictions, right or wrong. I admire this quality about you and Son both. But this thing, especially with the house, is getting out of control. I don't think Son's a lazy person or he's trying to take advantage of you. His problem is he got too much on his plate and doesn't know how to either balance it all or take some off."

I stared down at my phone, sitting near Frank's hip. The mother in me voted to snatch the phone and call Son. The wife in me voted to assure Frank that I trusted his judgment. The woman in me voted to rise up and rebel against my husband just 'cause we been doin' that since Adam and Eve; it's in our flesh nature. Two out of three in me was votin' to call Son.

Frank must have read my face, filled with indecision.

"B, I can't stop you from calling Son if you want to. I've already given you my advice."

I know Frank wasn't actually giving me the green light to call Son, but it wasn't the red light, either. It was more like the yellow light sayin' "go if you think you can make it."

So that time, the two out of three voices inside my head won the majority vote. I took the phone and went into the kitchen area of the hotel.

Frank turned the TV volume back up. Guess he didn't want to hear what I was about to say.

I called Son, only he didn't answer. I don't know if he was still mad from whatever was said between him and Frank or if he was truly unable to answer his phone.

I left him a message. "Son, this is your momma. I understand you're going to do whatever needs to be done at the house. I appreciate you. Take what you need from the account and keep all the receipts for the taxes. Don't let Ida Mae talk you down any more on the rent. I know you gon' do a good job. Me and

Frank gon' have a real good time this week. Got a full schedule. I'll give you a call later in the week if I can. But if I don't, don't you worry. I'll see you next week. Love you. Bye."

Glad to have this out of the way, I was getting my mouth ready to say a quick prayer and ask God to intervene when He all but stopped me with this thought: He didn't get to vote earlier when I was tallying up my thoughts and feelings and instincts; why was I involving Him now?

Forgive me, Lord. I gotta do better before I really mess something up.

5

I can't speak for Frank, but I wasn't prepared for all the food they had at the dinner. Kennedy had planned a family-style meal, so everything was spread out in front of us—fajita chicken, cheese, beef, steak, two different kinds of beans, guacamole, sour cream, pico de gallo, salsa, tortillas, and queso. Whew! And it all tasted so good, too. And I should know, seeing as I had a taste of everything they passed in front of my eyes!

About twelve of us enjoyed ourselves real good in our separate dining area. We was mostly making small talk, you know, seeing as we didn't all know each other. Seem like Kennedy and her two friends, who I found out were twins named Jordan and River, was more into talking about how fattening everything was, even though the bride-to-be must have picked out the menu.

Gary, Frank, and a few other men had a spirited conversation regarding sports, a topic about which my husband could talk non-stop for twenty-four hours, I am certain. Me and some of the other wives chit-chatted about how nice the rooms were and how beautiful our hotel was. Some of Dr. Westhouse's family members had driven in and joined us.

I figured out from the table conversation that Whitney and Kennedy were sisters. Couldn't tell from their looks, though—they had two totally different face shapes and tones. I wouldn't have guessed they was even from the same branch on the family tree, let alone sisters.

Anyway, the Whitney girl didn't have much in common with Kennedy and the landmark twins.

There was one young man in our party who seemed to stick out, too. Gary had introduced him earlier as the photographer. His name was Chad, and he was Gary's son's best friend.

"Oh, how nice!" I had remarked. "Will your son come later?" I had asked after the formal introductions were over and I had Dr. Westhouse's ear to myself and only a few other people.

He shook his head and said somberly, "No. He decided not to come."

"Okay," was all I knew to say. Got to be some

reason why a son won't come to his own father's wedding, but it wasn't none of my business. Good thing I hadn't asked in front of everybody.

Gary perked up. "But my dad will be here, and I'm super-excited about him coming."

"That's a blessing," I remarked. I almost said something about the father-son bond, but seeing as the third generation would be absent, I kept my mouth zipped while somebody else kindly changed the subject.

Anyhow, Chad took pictures nearly the whole time we ate, documenting everything like he was on assignment with the National Geographic.

About the time we'd whittled down most of the food, they started serving us cake. It was one of them Mexican cakes dipped in milk. I don't too much care for the texture, so Frank ate his and half of mine, too.

He was almost finished when we heard a shriek come from Whitney at her end of the table. "Oh my gosh! I just swallowed a bite—this has *milk* in it!"

"Duh! It's tres *leches* cake," Kennedy replied. She slammed her fork on the table and rushed to her sister's side.

"You *know* I'm allergic to milk!" Whitney yelled as though this might mean a death sentence.

My stomach tightened. I done seen a few reactions in my day—allergies ain't nothin' to play with.

"*You* know you're allergic to milk, too. Why did you eat it?"

By then, Kennedy was fishing through Whitney's purse. I could see a patch of red skin crawling up Whitney's neck.

Dr. Westhouse got up out of his seat, as did Frank and another doctor who was with us. If Whitney was going to have a medical emergency, she sure picked the right company to do it with.

Kennedy slammed a tube on the table. "Do you need it?"

"I don't know. I only had two bites," Whitney said. Her voice had a slight wheeze in it and the red patch was spreading up to her chin now. "Why did you order cake with milk when you know I can't eat it?"

My stomach-knot loosened 'cause that was a pretty long and petty sentence she sputtered out. She must not have been too bad off.

"I ordered what *I* wanted to eat because it's *my* wedding," Kennedy said.

"But I'm"—wheeze—"the maid of honor," Whitney panted. Her face was starting to swell.

"Whitney, stop talking," Frank said. "Catch your breath."

Whitney took hold of the chair's arms and closed her eyes. We were all silent, watching Whitney's skin calm down from red to pink and her breathing go from quick to almost normal.

41

"Good job," Frank coaxed. "Just relax. Is your throat or your tongue swelling?"

Whitney shook her head.

"Drama over!" Kennedy announced. "Thanks for ruining our first night on the beach, Whitney."

River and Jordan gave demeaning looks to Whitney as well.

Poor Whitney's eyes filled with tears.

"No," Dr. Westhouse stopped her. He and Frank were still standing over Whitney. "You *cannot* start crying. You might compromise your breathing."

Whitney blinked quickly. Swallowed hard. She took some sips of water. "I'm fine," she said to Frank and Gary. "Thank you."

We all waited a few more minutes, watching her color return and her chest resume a decent rate of heaving. A little small talk here and there eased the tension. When the doctors returned to their seats, I figured they must have been fairly certain Whitney was out of the woods.

"Are you finished stealing my spotlight?" Kennedy asked.

Whitney threw her dinner napkin on the table. "I'm out of the wedding," she managed to say in a breathy tone.

"Seriously? You can't drop out of my wedding. We won't have enough women to match the men."

"You'll survive." Whitney got up from the table and walked toward the lobby area.

I stood up to follow her 'cause it didn't look like anyone else was gonna go see about the chile. Who knows? She might have been made a turn for the worse as soon as she was out of sight.

Kennedy made a smacking sound when I went to tend to her sister. Now, it was one thing for her to sass her sister, but I ain't no kin to Miss Kennedy and I wasn't scared of her. I held up my index finger. "Looka here. I don't know what caused you to wake up on the wrong side of the bed this morning, but you not gon' treat me any kind of way. I'm an *invited guest*. I didn't travel all this way to be disrespected."

Kennedy sucked in her lip. "Yes, ma'am."

Them wonder twins sat there with their eyes all bucked out.

The only person I cared about at the moment was Frank. He had a little smirk on his face like he was right proud of me. That was all I needed to see.

I snatched the allergy medicine off the table, then left out the private dining room, chasin' after Whitney. Finally caught up with her in the hotel lobby. From the way she had plopped into one of the spitfire leather chairs, I could tell she was still tryin' to regulate her breathing.

"You need to sit down for a second 'cause all this

speed-walking ain't helping your lungs right now, honey." I handed her the medicine.

"Thank you."

"You're welcome. Now just steady yourself. Breathe in and out, nice and slow. I'm gonna help you get to your room."

"Okay."

Frank came over to us and asked if I was planning on coming back to the dinner.

"No, honey, I'm tired from the flight. I'm going on back to our hotel room once I see Whitney to hers."

"You sure?"

"Yes. I'll be fine." God is God all over the world. His protection be the same no matter where you are. "Go on and enjoy some more time with your friends."

"Long as you stay put and don't get back out by yourself," Frank warned, I guess because that's what men do.

"I'll text you as soon as I get back to the room," I assured him.

With that, Frank was satisfied to leave me and Whitney together.

She and I caught one of those little shuttles back to the Rockefeller building. Once in our building, we made our way to the elevator well. I kept one hand on her back as we waited for the elevator. Wanted to feel her breathing. I had also started praying for her silently 'cause I got the feeling her problems was more than physical. She and her sister had been going at each other's throats since we landed.

When the elevator opened, we stepped on. Whitney pushed the number nine. In the silence, with just the two of us on the elevator, I heard her sniffing. Crying. The Lord knows I got a soft spot in my heart for young folk 'cause they don't know no better. You really can't get mad at folk who ain't lived long enough to realize that there ain't nothing new under the sun. Far as they can tell, everything is brand new and critical.

"How long you and your sister been feuding?"

She wiped her eyes. "Forever."

I chuckled. "Yeah. I had a sister. We used to fight when we were younger, too."

"When did the fighting stop?"

"When one of us finally had enough. It takes two to argue, you know?"

"You sound like our mom."

"Your mother is right. Is she coming to the wedding?"

"No." Whitney wiped her eyes. "She passed away ten years ago."

I shook my head. What a hard blow for the girls that must have been. "I'm so—"

"Don't be sorry. My mom wouldn't have come to this stupid wedding anyway."

"Oh. And why do you say that?" I had my own

reasons why the wedding was silly, but I wanted to hear hers since we were on the same team.

"My mom wouldn't have come because she was afraid to fly on planes," Whitney explained.

I was glad I kept my mouth shut this time, too, 'cause I surely wasn't expecting her answer.

"What about your father? Is he coming?"

"My dad left my mom when I was, like five. I've only seen him three times since then. We don't invite him to things because we know he won't show up. Why waste the stamp or the time it takes to type his email address for an Evite, you know?"

"You got a point."

The elevator dinged and we got off. I followed Whitney down the hallway to the right, studying her walk all the way. She seemed to be back to normal now. No wobbling. No dragging her feet. And her speech on the ride up had been totally fine. Her face was puffy, but some of that might have been from her crying. And the splotchy marks on her face and neck had almost disappeared.

She stopped at Room 9221. I made a mental note, so I could call her later.

"Look like you gonna be all right now, Whitney."

"Yes, I think so. Thank you so much for making sure I made it back safely, Ms....I'm sorry, what's your name again?"

"Pretty much everybody calls me Mama B."

"Mama B. Well, it's too bad my own sister didn't care enough to make sure I'm alive."

I glared at her. "Now, you know better than I do that your sister cares about you."

She snarled her face. "What makes you so sure?"

"'Cause the second you said something about swallowing milk, Kennedy was the *first* one at your side. Honey, she beat a whole slew of doctors to an emergency situation!"

Whitney paused for a second. "I guess."

"Mmmm hmmm. Your sister might be actin' some kind of funny right now, but when it really counted, Kennedy was there for you. Think on that tonight instead of all those bad thoughts about whatever happened between y'all in the past, you hear?"

"I'll try. But don't get your hopes up. My sister is impossible." She withdrew her key from a pocket in her skirt, then swiped the key in front of the door's sensor. The door buzzed softly and she opened it.

"Thanks again, Mama B."

I winked at her. "Good night, Whitney."

"Good night."

I kept my promise to Frank and let him know when I made it back to our quarters, then I got myself ready for a good night's sleep in that soft, pretty bed.

I called Whitney's room just before I went to sleep. All was well on her end, so I drifted off.

Frank came in a little after midnight. He must

have had a glass of wine or something because I heard him in there brushing his teeth for quite a while. He know I can't stand the smell of alcohol on nobody's breath, let alone somebody who's about to kiss me goodnight.

Come to think of it, me and Frank had a lot of little things we had to learn to overlook in each other, so long as the Lord wasn't pressing the issue. Being married again had taught me to understand the difference between what was a sin unto God versus an annoyance unto me. Frank had showed me clear as day in the Scriptures that having a drink wasn't a sin —being *drunk* was.

I stuck to my guns that you can't get drunk without taking a drink in the first place and it's best to not even start going down a road that can lead to disaster. I ain't never been drunk, but I imagine it's a fine line between drinking and gettin' drunk, and the last person to be a good judge is the one with the beer in his hand.

So me and Frank don't agree on that one and we probably never will.

When Frank finally came out of the restroom, he didn't get in the bed. He stood over me and kissed my cheek. "B, you up?"

"A little." I opened my eyes and saw him standing there, fully dressed.

Frank sighed. "I got something to ask you."

I looked at him. "What is it?"

"Actually...ummm...all right. Whitney has dropped out of the wedding for good. Will you stand in her place?"

"What?!" I sat straight up. "Did you drink a little too much tonight?"

"No, I did not."

The whites of his eyes still had their normal color and his words weren't running together, so I took it he was sober, even though the question that had come from his lips sounded like he was sloppy drunk.

"Let me try talking to Whitney," I offered instead. "I'm sure I can get her to—"

"Kennedy doesn't want her in the wedding now."

"That's nonsense, Frank. They're sisters. They'll work something out. They gonna have to because I can't be in the wedding."

"You *can't* or you *won't*?"

"I mean I *can't* and I *ain't*. You know how I felt about this entire wedding from way back at the airport. I'm only here for the scenery and to spend time with you."

There was a knock at the door. Frank whispered. "That would be Kennedy."

"What she doin' at our door?" I whisper-shouted back.

"She's about to ask you what I already asked you," he said. "I just wanted to give you a heads-up."

My mouth flew open wide. I fussed as much as I could without her hearing me on the other side of the door. "Why didn't you tell her already that adding me to the wedding was a terrible idea?"

"I can't speak for you, B. Sometimes right when I think you're going to turn somebody down, you get an unction from the Lord to say yes. No telling how the Lord is using you tonight."

There Frank went again, bringing the Lord into my decisions. Now, I wasn't no stranger to lettin' the Lord have His way in my life. But something like this seemed like an automatic understood 'no' to me; wasn't no need in wastin' a good prayer to the Lord on this here situation.

Knock knock came again.

Frank got up to answer the door. I went to the restroom, so I could grab the hotel's terrycloth robe and put it around myself. I caught my reflection in the mirror. The worry lines, the sour expression—didn't look nothin' like my normal self. *What exactly am I mad at? 'Cause my husband didn't shut down their request? 'Cause I still didn't like the age gap?*

I couldn't give an answer right away. What I *did* know was that the scowl on my face was not a good look, and the mindset behind that scowl had no business running my mouth.

"Lord, You know I don't want to be in this wedding. You know my feelings. You know I didn't come here to work." I sighed. Just listening to myself pray, the words was all about me, my, and I, a sure sign I wasn't yielded to His will. It ain't no sense in somebody prayin' and askin' God to get involved if they done already made up they mind to do what they wanna do no matter what anyhow.

I bowed my head and finished the prayer the same way Jesus did before He went to the cross. The same way I always do before God signs me up for something I didn't see on the horizon. "Nevertheless, not my will but thy will be done."

6

"Hi. Miss B?"

"Mama B," I corrected Kennedy.

"May I speak to you? It'll only take a minute," she pleaded, grabbing a handful of her own hair and pulling down the sides like she was making a ponytail on either side. I suppose that was supposed to make me think of her as a child or something—I don't know. That was a new move on me, but I wasn't falling for it.

Everything in me wanted to say 'don't even waste your baby-breath', but I kept my sly words to myself and kept my eyes from rollin' at her. "Go 'head, chile."

Frank took my words as his cue to step out on the balcony. He shut the sliding door behind him, leaving me and Kennedy alone. I led her to the dinette table and we both sat down.

"My sister dropped out of the wedding," she started, "and I was wondering. I mean, well, let me back up and say that You. Are. A. *Beautiful* Woman."

"Thank you."

"You're fashionable. Your hair is beautiful, your makeup is flawless. And you're the perfect size."

Somebody sure taught this girl the art of flattery.

"I was wondering if you could fill in the wedding party, since my sister dropped out."

"Well, let me back up and ask first, did your sister really mean she wasn't going to be in the wedding?"

"Yes. She's...I don't want to talk about her." Kennedy blinked rapidly.

I must say I was surprised to see the water pooling in her eyes. Guess I shouldn't have been shocked, though. People who treat others bad be the main ones cryin' theyself to sleep every night. One of my aunts was like that—meaner than a one-eyed rattlesnake— always on the defensive, striking at any and everybody in her vicinity. She never did get no Jesus or no counselin'. Over the years, she got worse and worse. It's too many folk like her walking around undiagnosed. They need a lot of love and a lot of help, and some of that help need to come from the mental health doctors.

Anyhow, now that me and Kennedy was by ourselves for the first time, without her crew and even without Gary, I saw her with fresh eyes. Her voice was quieter. Her face softer. Mind you, she was there to ask me a favor; it was in her best interest to be polite and all. But I discerned her genuine heart—the one she showed when she wasn't around all the people she was tryin' so hard to impress.

I put my hand over Kennedy's to stop her from wringing them. "Honey, I'm sure Whitney would change her mind if you two would sit down and talk."

Now she had tears to wipe. Whew! These two sisters was not gonna worry me!

"No. I can't talk to her. After this trip, our sisterhood is done."

I tsked. "Don't even say such a thing, Kennedy. Sisters are for life. I bet you and Whitney been through a lot together, huh?"

"I went through a lot with her. She's always had it easy." Kennedy pouted.

"Aaah. So you're the oldest?"

"How'd you know?"

"'Cause that's how it always is in a family. The oldest one ends up taking responsibility for the younger ones. I can't rightly say it's fair, but it's the way roles tend to pan out."

"Well, it's a terrible paradigm," Kennedy said matter-of-factly. "Someone needs to fix it."

I couldn't stop myself from laughing at her observation. Thankfully, she cracked a smile, too.

"When God makes a person, He puts them exactly

where they need to be. Even if the family ain't ready for 'em, even if He knows the family's going to have turmoil, He builds people and flowers and animals to thrive wherever He puts 'em, whether it be the desert or the rainforest," I told her.

She bit her bottom lip. "And I'm thinking He put you here to be in my wedding." She flashed a bright smile.

I frowned. Blinked my eyes slowly. "You a smart cookie, you know?"

"Is that a yes?"

"No."

Her face and her shoulders collapsed. "But I *need* you." She stamped her foot.

"What you *need* is to stop prancin' around here like a diva, go apologize to your sister, and get this wedding back on track again. I can help you with *that* if you want me to."

Kennedy slapped her own forehead. "This is a total disaster."

"There you go getting all dramatic again." I pulled her hand off her face and looked her square in the eyes. "Kennedy, you about to be a grown and married woman. Married to a doctor, at that. It's gonna be a lot of compromises up ahead because he's partly dedicated to saving lives. You can't be falling apart every time something don't go your way."

While I had her ear, I really wanted to talk to her

about a whole bunch of other stuff, namely, why on earth she was marryin' a man twice her age and who were these petty so-called friends of hers. But I could see from the way her eyebrows cinched together she had enough to chew on for a while. "You think you up to talking to your sister tonight?"

She closed her eyes and nodded.

"Good. You believe in God?"

Her eyes popped open. "Of course."

"Then let's pray and ask Him to soften Whitney's heart and give you the right words."

I didn't give her no chance to think about it. I started in with the prayer, asking the Lord to remind both sisters of their forgiving hearts and cause Kennedy's words to bring about peace. "In Jesus's name. Amen."

"Amen," Kennedy agreed.

She stood. "I'll let you know how it goes. And thank you, Mama B."

"You're welcome." I walked her to the door. "Have a good night."

"You, too."

Frank must have been listening to the entire conversation because he come back in the room with a huge grin on his face. "You dodged the bullet that time, B!"

"No thanks to you!" I laughed.

He wrapped me up in a big hug. "I knew you would know how to handle it. You always do."

WE WAS SCHEDULED to meet up for a snorkeling excursion after breakfast Tuesday morning, according to the itinerary. I was fine with the customized omelets at the buffet, but that snorkeling thing wasn't nowhere near my bucket list.

"Awww, B. You sure you don't wanna try something new?" Frank asked again as he set a glass of cranberry juice near my plate.

"No, sirree. I'll sit back on the sidelines and watch y'all have fun," I said. I took a sip of the juice and ate a bit more of my spinach, chicken, and cheese omelet. "This sure is delicious." And the sweet breeze flowing through the open windows only added to the mood.

"I'm going to go back for a waffle," Frank said.

"Sounds good."

He left me at our table for two. I could see almost everybody in our party scattered around the dining area. Everybody except Whitney. I was hoping Kennedy would come over and give me a good report. She was too caught up in her conversation with Jordan and River, however. Gary was making his rounds, speaking to all the wedding guests. He had already come by our table and made sure we were enjoying ourselves.

My cell phone vibrated on the table. Now, Frank had already told me I didn't need to carry it with me so long as we were together. Old habits die hard, though.

When I saw it was Son on the line, I hurried up and answered. Frank's waffle wasn't going to take forever.

"Hi, Son."

"Hello."

"How you doin'?"

"Fine. You having a good time in Miami Beach?"

"Oh, it's amazing. You and Wanda gonna have to come here sometime."

He cleared his throat. "Momma, you have got to do something about Frank."

"Something like what?"

"Tell him to stay out of *Jackson* business," Son said. "If he wasn't married to you, I would have told him where to get off yesterday."

"Well, he *is* married to me. And I'm a Jackson-*Wilson* now. I got to look out for what's best for *both* of us."

"What about me? Am I not in the picture anymore? What about what's best for me and *my* family?"

"What do you want, Son? The house? I already told you it was yours soon as you ready to start payin' the taxes and insurance. You gonna need about six thousand dollars in January."

"I'm not in a position to pay that kind of money right now," he said.

"Well, how long will it take you to *get* yourself in position?"

He mumbled, "I don't know."

"Two years? Five years?"

"I said I don't know. I guess I was thinking we'd have enough to take care of the house when you...you know...when we get the insurance money."

My lungs tightened. "Oh, so you waitin' on me to die. And in the meantime, you want me and Frank to struggle with the upkeep and the tenants and the paperwork during our golden years, right?"

"I mean...me and Wanda just don't have the money right now. Maybe, I don't know, in another ten years or so..."

Frank was still standing in line, so I had plenty of time to give Son a piece of my mind. "Son, you know you ain't bit mo' plannin' to get ready to take over the house. You drivin' a brand new Escalade and Wanda drivin' a Jaguar. Y'all spendin' plenty money on them cars and your fine clothes. You done worked yourself into a lifestyle where you got to spend two and three hours a day goin' back and forth to work 'cause you couldn't afford to wait a month or two to find something more suitable.

That means y'all was livin' check to check, ain't hardly put away nothing for a rainy day. But that's y'all's business. I tell you this, though: I'm seventy-five and I figure I got a good twenty years left at least. You and Wanda gonna have to come up with a better retirement plan than hittin' a jackpot when I kick the bucket!"

"Momma, I'm not saying—"

"That *is* what you said, Son!" My hands were shaking so bad I could hardly hold the phone. I know I'm going to die one day and I'm well prepared. But I found it quite insulting to think that my family was planning how to spend my money while the blood was still running warm in my veins. This was worse than the prodigal son asking his father for his inheritance decades ahead of time.

I had lost track of Frank's whereabouts at the buffet. Shoot, I had lost track of all my senses by that point. "Son, I'm going to hang up now. Don't call me no more while I'm on this trip. Frank done already told you the same."

"Frank is not my father."

"Well, if you—"

"B, you all right?" I felt Frank's hand on my back.

"Bye," I said to Son and then slammed my phone face down on the table. I folded my arms across my chest.

"What's wrong?"

My lips bunched up in a mean pucker. Might as

well tell the truth. "That was Son on the phone."

Frank sat down and started eating as though I hadn't even spoken.

"You ain't got nothin' to say? Especially after you told him not to call."

"Naw," Frank shrugged. "Soon as I told him to let us be for the week, you called him right back so..."

I couldn't even argue with the man.

I was tired of Frank being right about everything, though. Hadn't he ever made a mistake with his children? Hadn't he ever made a bad decision? *Sittin' over there eatin' that waffle like he Mr. Perfect, blaming me for Son's issues.*

I wasn't in no mood for jet-skiing or jet-ski-watchin', either. "You know what? I think I'm just going to skip the excursion. I'll meet up with you all for lunch."

"B. No. We talked about this," Frank said. "Don't let what's happening at home interfere with what's happening on our vacation." He took my phone, turned it off, and put it in the front pocket of his khaki shirt. "No. More. Phone calls."

I blew out a cleansing breath. *Lord Jesus, help.* Ignoring the calls wouldn't ease my mind. Wouldn't take back Son's hurtful words.

Being holed up in my hotel room wouldn't help none, either.

"Okay. I'll go."

"Thank you, B. I really want us to make some lasting memories here this week. Leave all the rest of that alone. Tomorrow has enough worries of its own."

"Matthew, Chapter six," I said. My husband knows the Word of God always brings me comfort.

Frank added, "Verse thirty-four."

7

All these water adventures on the agenda was appropriate for the beach, I suppose, but I just wasn't the one. Didn't stop Frank from signing up to jet ski Wednesday. Seem like the kid in him came out, just skitting across the water. He waved at me a few times and I waved back from the comfort of my chair perched on the beach under a big, blue umbrella.

Frank's wide smiles reminded me of a boy on a ten-speed bike. And that started me to thinking about Son and when he was a child. Albert made all of our kids work for things, but at the end of the day, so long as they did what they were told and kept their grades up in school, we didn't have much of a reason to say 'no' to what they asked for. Back then, we didn't have all this internet shopping and reality TV shows with celebrities buying thousand dollar blankets for their dogs. Kids didn't know to ask for anything more than what their peers had. In Son's case, all he wanted was name-brand tennis shoes and video games. When he got old enough for a job, Albert made him buy his own shoes and whatnots.

Everything changes, of course, when kids have to spend their own money. I remember one time Son refused to buy a box of cereal because I didn't have a coupon for it.

Tickled me just thinking about it again, even after all these years.

"What's funny?"

I looked to my right and saw Whitney standing tall beside me.

"Just thinking about old times. Grab one of them chairs." I motioned toward empty chairs a few feet away. "Come rest your feet with me."

She joined me with a seat of her own under the umbrella.

"You didn't want to get on the jet ski?"

"No." She rubbed her belly. "Upset stomach. Plus I'm notorious for ear infections. Plus my allergies. If something weird touches me, I might explode."

"Oh. I understand." The she talk, it was almost like listenin' to Ophelia back when we was younger. She used to claim every illness in the book until Pastor started teaching us different.

"So you ain't gonna get in water none this week?"

"Probably not. Beaches, water, sand...not my thing."

"Well, I understand about the beaches and the water. You know, us black women...we don't hardly believe in getting our hair wet," I told her.

She peered at me. "Why not?"

"Too much work to get it back straight."

"If I were black, there's no way I'd wear my hair straight. I'd have, like, the biggest afro." She held her hands beside her head and patted her imaginary afro. "Like Thelma from Good Times."

I poked my lips out. "What you know 'bout Good Times, Miss Whitney?"

"I know a lot about Good Times," she insisted. "My mom used to watch that show. It was her favorite. She used to watch all those '70s shows on the throw-back networks. My mom was, like, a *real* Christian lady. She liked them because there wasn't a lot of violence or profanity. Kennedy and I would beg her to change the channel."

I laughed. "Your mother must have been a fun person."

"She was." Whitney gazed at the ocean. "She was eccentric, she was strong, she was vibrant. Smart. Outspoken. Loved by everyone. She was, like, everything I'm not."

"How you figure you nothin' like her?"

"Kennedy's the one she adored. She and mom were a lot alike. I've always been the wild, weird one."

"Just 'cause your mother's personality matched your sister's more don't mean she didn't love you, too."

Whitney shook her head. "You know that necklace Kennedy wears? The one with the blue beads and the shells and the silver balls on it? She wears it everywhere."

Now that Whitney mentioned it, I did remember seeing it on her sister's neck. "Believe I do."

"My mom wore it all the time, too. She gave it to Kennedy before she died," Whitney said.

I tried to reason, "Well, maybe she knew how much Kennedy loved the necklace."

Whitney smacked her lips. "It's not just the necklace. There's like, a buncha stuff my mom didn't leave for me."

"Maybe she left it in Kennedy's care, but I'm sure your sister would share some things if you asked her."

Whitney shook her head again. "Kennedy's always been the golden child. But I'm okay with it. Somebody has to be the black sheep, right? No offense."

"None taken." I wasn't quite sure what else to say to this gal. Look like she was dead set on getting the short end of the stick.

"Well," I said then sighed, "give it some time. One of these days you'll wake up and realize your mother gave you a lot more than you knew. She gave you love and shared her faith with you, and that's the most valuable thing a mother can give to her child. You don't grow up around someone that special without a piece of them rubbing off on you."

"I'm still thinking she rubbed it all on Kennedy."

"Awww...you'll see soon enough. And one day, years from now, you and Kennedy will look back at these wedding pictures and tell your daughters the funny story about how you almost weren't in the wedding, but you two worked things out."

"We haven't worked anything out," Whitney snapped. "I'm not in the wedding. I'm trying my best to stay away from her the rest of this trip."

"Didn't Kennedy come and talk to you?"

"Uh, no. She's done nothing but hang out with River and Jordan. She's posted a zillion pictures on Instagram."

Well, tell me something.

"Did she *say* she'd talked to me?"

"Not exactly," I admitted. "It was just something we discussed."

"Wait...she talked to you about me? What did she say?"

"Wasn't no gossip, chile. Mostly I was asking her questions, trying to get to the bottom of what's going on with you two. Shame you done came all the way out here to be in the wedding and now you two done fell out to the point where you not even gonna be in the ceremony."

Whitney shook her head. She studied the ocean waves for a moment. "My sister's not, like, an evil person. She's just...wrong."

"There's a mighty big difference between evil and wrong," I agreed. "I'm glad you recognize. That'll help you keep on loving her no matter what. Now, I want you to tell me what you reckon is really going on with you and your sister."

"What I *reckon*?"

"What you *think* happened between you and her?" I rephrased. Forgot I was talking to a millennial.

Whitney sighed. "I was thirteen when my mom first got sick. Kennedy was sixteen, and she kind of became my mom's caregiver. She also suddenly became my mom. That's when everything between me and Kennedy changed. She got bossy and mean and offensive."

Right then, the Holy Spirit started giving me an understanding to where everything Whitney said, He was telling me Kennedy's side of the story at the same time.

"Sounds to me like your sister was scared, over-whelmed, and in survival mode. Think about it. Sixteen years old. You're supposed to be worryin' about your prom dress or your driver's license. Your sister was worryin' about what would become of her mother's life, and probably yours, too. 'Specially since your daddy was long gone by then."

She stared down at the sand. "I never really thought of it like that. Kennedy's always been so strong."

Spoken like a true little sister who looked up to her big sister. My heart started melting for them two girls. They'd already lost their parents. I couldn't sit by and watch them lose each other, too.

"Excuse me," a male voice came from behind us.

Whitney and I turned to find the photographer boy behind us.

"Do you know what time they're coming in from jet-skiing?"

I pulled the program from my sling purse. "Eleven-thirty."

"Thank you."

Now, his words were meant for me, but his eyes were on Whitney.

"Um...I've got about thirty minutes before I can take more pictures. You want to go get a drink? Maybe take a dip in the water?"

Whitney was suddenly healed of all disease and set free from fear of water. She rose from her chair and started walking off with Chad.

Left me slamp by myself!

Me and the Lord had a good laugh about them two. The way they was looking at each other, I wouldn't be surprised if we was back at the beach next year for their wedding.

Frank and the others finally came back to shore about half an hour later. My husband was about two shades darker after being out there in the sun so long. Matter-of-fact, so was everybody else. Kennedy, Gary, the healing waters twins, all of them.

"Whew!" Frank yelled. "That was exhilarating!"

"Nothing like it!" Kennedy agreed. "Mama B, you missed out on all the fun."

"I'm sure y'all had enough for me, too."

Kennedy asked, "You didn't snorkel with us yesterday, and you didn't jet-ski with us today. Are you going to do *anything* on the agenda, Mama B?"

"Oh, I'll be at all the meals," I assured her. "But I don't fool around with water too much."

"Can't you swim?" she pressed.

"I can doggie paddle over to the side of a pool like the one at our house. But seeing as this is the ocean, wouldn't be no ledge for me to grab hold to."

"B, I didn't know you couldn't *swim* swim," Frank said with an astonished look on his face.

"You never asked."

They finished toweling off and we all started walking back toward the shuttle pick-up spot. They was all just-a laughin' and teasin' each other about what they'd experienced out on the water. Kennedy and her friends walked in their row of three while the rest of us—except Gary, obviously—was coupled up.

Dr. Westhouse was the odd man out. I almost felt sorry for him. Almost. Not all the way, though, because that's what you get when you tryin' to marry somebody you ain't got nothin' in common with. I still hadn't seen them two snuggling up together or looking at each other with goo-goo eyes like you'd expect to see with a couple about to tie the knot. Kennedy seemed to be doing her best to entertain the twins instead of spend time with her soon-to-be husband. And wasn't nobody sayin' nothin'! Nobody except Whitney, but she was doin' all her talking behind Kennedy's back.

8

_____

M e and Frank took advantage of our only "on your own" day by sleeping in late. Instead of breakfast, we had a light brunch around ten o'clock. Then Frank invited me to a walk along the shore.

A day like this at a place like this deserved a long walk. "Love to."

Hand-in-hand, we walked from the Rockefeller to the trolley stop. We sat, snuggled up to one another like newleyweds, all the way to the beach. When our feet hit the sand again, we took off our shoes, enjoying the feel of sand between our toes. The beach wasn't as crowded as it probably would be later today, when people who wanted strong tans came out to bathe in the sun's rays.

The sand turned to slush the closer we got to the

waterline. Cool, wet earth beneath our feet. Water lapping at our ankles. The constant sound of tumbling waves. Fresh air filling our lungs.

I squeezed Frank's hand. "This place is beautiful."

"Yes, indeed."

I wanted to ask Frank if he'd seen what I'd seen with Kennedy and Gary. Which basically means I wanted to gossip. Only I didn't want to ruin the good mood we was both in.

Frank and I strolled along the beach silently for several hundred feet.

"I understand why folk retire here," Frank said. "Plenty sunshine. Good food. You notice how friendly everybody is?"

"Yes. But folks back home is friendly, too," I reminded him.

"I suppose. There's something relaxing about this place, though. The beauty of it makes you stop and realize how magnificent the Earth is, reflecting God's glory."

A tiny bird landed about ten feet ahead of us. He wasn't scared of us, I gathered by how close we were to him. He burrowed down with his beak, found whatever it was he was looking for in the sand, and took off again.

"Wish things could be this peaceful all the time. Cares of this life get in the way, though," I remarked.

"You see what that bird did?" Frank asked. "He

flew down, got what God had provided in the moment, and left without a care in the world. Should be the same for us, too."

We kept walking, both of us thinking about what he'd said, I'm sure. Slow, easy steps massaged by the tide. The sun was still high. The day ahead of us long. Contrarily, Frank and I were staring our own life's sunsets in the face.

"You thinking about the house?" I asked.

"No. I'm thinking about us. Here."

"Here?"

"Well, maybe not here. Some place *like* Miami Beach."

"Are you talking about moving?"

"Not any time soon."

I stopped. "Frank. I've lived near Peasner all my adult life and I ain't never had thoughts about moving away from my family. Where is this idea of moving coming from?"

Frank stopped, too. Looked down at me. "I talked to Frank, Jr. Before we left. Told him I needed to change some things in the will so you'd be taken care of in the event something happens to me."

"Okaaay."

"Seems he and Son have been sipping on the same batch of crazy Kool-Aid."

"What'd he say?"

"Pretty much everything Son said. That I'm brainwashed. Selfish. Not thinking clearly. He threatened to have me evaluated by a psychologist," Frank said.

The strain on my husband's face nearly broke my heart in two. "Oh, Frank, I'm so sorry." I pulled him into a hug. Lord knows, I always thought when the kids left the house, we wouldn't have to worry with them no more. This season of life, however, comes with another set of parent-child challenges me and Frank wasn't ready for.

"I didn't raise my kids to argue over money," he spoke into my shoulder.

"Me, either, Frank."

Frank held on to me tighter. "This is not what their mother and I instilled in them."

"I know it ain't." Bad as this sounds, I was glad my kids weren't the only ones actin' up, though.

Frank raised off of me, wiping his eyes.

My Lord. I do believe that was the first time I'd actually seen Frank cry. "You gonna be all right?"

"*We're* gonna be all right," he said. He led me as we started walking again, the waves lapping at our feet. "Maybe, in the next five years or so, we should strongly consider liquidating our assets, consolidating our funds, and living off the interest in a different location. When we're both dead and gone, we can leave the principal to all our kids. Simple."

"No, it ain't simple. Your two was lookin' forward to a 50-50 split of your inheritance. Now they got to split it six ways, and you puttin' more into the pot than me. That's not fair to Frank Jr. and Eva."

"What's not fair is them feeling entitled to what they didn't even earn."

"You know it's honorable for a man to leave an inheritance to his children," I reminded my husband of the Word.

"It's also honorable for a son to honor his father's second wife. He should treat you the exact same way he would treat his own mother if she were alive and we were still married. I wouldn't expect him to come pull the rug out from under her, if something happened to me."

"But I'm *not* his mother, Frank. This is a whole different situation."

"Emotionally, yes. Legally, no."

I shook my head softly. "You got to consider people's feelings sometimes, baby. It ain't always about money or facts. You're correct about the law. The question is: Are you willing to lose the relationship with your children over it?"

Two seagulls cawed as though calling a truce to our disagreement.

Frank embraced me again. "I guess moving here was wishful thinking. Must just be the waves talking."

"Much as I like this scenery, I don't think running away from home is the answer," I told him. "Since neither one of us wants to leave the other one on this earth with a fight on their hands, we're gonna have to fight together now. We need to sit these grown children down and tell them how the cow ate the cabbage. In a nice way."

His chest bounced with laughter. "Yes, in a nice way."

"It's a hard discussion, but it's got to be had."

Frank stood erect. "I don't see this as a discussion. It's an informational meeting, where we *tell* them what's going to happen in due time."

"We got to be open to suggestions," I said.

"Oh. Right. And feelings."

"Sentiment, Frank."

He rolled his eyes playfully.

"Feelings, whoah, whoah, whoah feelings," I sang off-tune deliberately, which caused my husband to chuckle loudly.

"B. What would I do without you?"

"Ain't no tellin'."

He put his arm around my shoulder. "We'd better head on back."

As we made a U-turn and walked back toward the shuttle station, out the corner of my eye, I saw what looked like a hand flailing in the water. I squinted my eyes to be sure. "Frank, you see that?"

"See what?"

I pointed toward the spot where I'd seen the hands, only there were four hands waving frantically now instead of two, about 300 yards away, I'm guessing. "Look like somebody's trying to get our attention."

We both walked into the water a bit to get just a teensy bit closer. The waves were crashing against nearby rocks, so it was hard to hear. But I put my hand behind my ear to tune in and heard a clear cry.

"Help us!"

"My Lord! They stranded in the water!"

Frank took off running toward the nearest life-guard tower.

I crossed my arms over my head three times to let them know we had seen them. "Hold on!" I yelled. "We're getting help." I'm guessing they understood because they stopped wasting their precious energy tryin' to get my attention. At least I prayed that was the reason they'd stopped moving in the water.

9

The lifeguard swam out with a floating device hanging from around his neck. By that time, people had gathered around me and started asking questions. About twenty or so of us watched as the guard pulled the swimmers back to shore. We cheered them on as the three of them got closer and closer.

Seem like out of nowhere, a camera crew showed up and started filming the rescue.

About fifty yards out, we could see it was a man and a woman. A minute later, I knew exactly who they were. "Frank, that's Whitney! And the photography boy!"

"Sure is."

Once they got about twenty feet or so away, a bunch of people ran into the water to help them the last bit of the way. They were obviously exhausted. Huffing and coughing, but still alive.

Thank You, Father.

There was another round of cheering for the guard when he finally stepped on shore.

"Just doin' my job, folks," he said. He asked Whitney and Chad if they were okay as he gave them bottles of water.

They nodded, tore into the drinks, and thanked the lifeguard over and over again.

"Oh my gosh, we almost died," Whitney yelled dramatically.

Chad put his arm around her. "We're okay."

The camera crew rushed toward Whitney, asking ridiculously obvious questions like "Were you scared for your life?" Whitney ate up the attention, clutching invisible pearls, animating every word with some kind of facial- or hand-expression. "It was terrible! Absolutely horrifying! My life flashed before my eyes!"

Chad's answers weren't quite as newsworthy, so the news crew focused on Whitney again as she retold the story. "I'm here for my sister's wedding. Our dad left us. Our mom died ten years ago. We're all we have left."

If I didn't know any better, I'd think the girl had practiced this story.

Whitney tore away from him and rushed to me. "Mama B! Thank God you saw us!" She squished her wet body into me. "This lady here is the real hero. She's my true angel!" Whitney kissed my cheek.

The crowd went, "Aaaah." I could see the feel-good headline already: Elderly woman saves girl at secluded section of Miami Beach. This was probably gonna go viral. Good thing I hadn't gotten my hair all wet.

Nevertheless, I answered Whitney, "I'm just thankful I saw your little skinny arms out there in the middle of the ocean." Despite the fact that she was messing up my new caftan dress, I squeezed her back.

Chad joined our group hug. "I can't thank you enough. Our board got swept away by this humongous wave. We swam back as far as we could, but we didn't have the energy to keep going. We must have been out there yelling for help for, like, fifteen minutes. No one heard or saw us except you."

Frank rubbed Chad's back. "Son, that was a miracle. Thank God."

"I do. I'm soooooo thankful. He saved us."

Whitney looked at Chad. They fell into a heap of emotion and hugs, holding on to one another. The crowd clapped this time.

"Let's get on back to the hotel," Frank suggested. "You two have had quite an ordeal. You need some rest." He waved off the camera crew. Just as quickly as they had come, they were off. I suppose they needed to get back and make a television story of things.

The four of us walked back to the shuttle as two couples arm-in-arm. When we reached the Rockefeller, Frank and I walked them to the elevators.

"Come on back down as soon as you can for lunch," I mothered them.

"I'm not hungry," Whitney said.

"Neither am I," from Chad.

"You need to replenish your nourishment," Frank advised. "You both look a little pale to me. If you're too tired, have them bring something to your rooms."

"Yes, sir," Chad agreed.

We all hugged one last time at Whitney's insistence, then they got on an elevator and left.

I started praying for her in my heart again because even though she liked the attention of the media, I know these frightening experiences can really shake a person up.

The time when my youngest son, Otha, got into a little motorcycle accident, I didn't think he was going to operate a vehicle again. Now, I didn't have no problem with him giving up motorcycles—them things so dangerous. But when he had all these other people drivin' him around town because he was too scared to take the wheel, I had to go into intercession for him as well as arrange a little situation where he didn't have no choice but to drive. I couldn't have my baby son crippled for life on account of a bad memory.

Whitney had already lost her mother and pretty much her father. Last thing she needed was to fear losing her own life, even though she wasn't in danger anymore.

That's how the enemy works, you know. He make you scared of stuff that *almost* happened so you won't appreciate what actually *is* happening. He don't want you to put two and two together and figure out it was God protecting you the first time, and it'll be God protecting you your whole life, filtering out what He won't allow to kill you from the stuff that He will allow to build you.

So, yeah, Whitney needed prayer.

10

————

We was back on the whirlwind agenda Friday morning. To my surprise, Kennedy and Gary was actually sitting by one another at one of the dining room tables for breakfast. Alone. No twins, no one else from our entourage around.

This was the perfect time to find out what was really going on with the two of them.

"Oh, there's Kennedy and Dr. Westhouse over there." I tipped my head in their direction.

Frank frowned as he craned his neck to look at their table. "Looks like they've almost finished their plates. Let's not disturb them."

"Nonsense, Frank. We'll have them all to ourselves."

I weaved my way over to their table before Frank

could firmly object. "Gary. Kennedy. So good to see you. Yesterday was quite the adventure, huh, with Whitney's incident at the beach."

Kennedy's face filled with concern. "Wait, what happened? Is she okay?"

"She is now. But she and Chad had to struggle to stay above water for a while there. Lifeguard had to swim out and get them. Thank God Frank found one quickly," I filled her in. "I missed the news last night, but they were probably on it."

"That doesn't make sense. Whitney's a strong swimmer."

My eyebrows squished together. "Your sister told me that she doesn't even like to get near water."

"She was All-American swimmer in high school. There's no way she let the tide carry her beyond her control."

Gary countered, "She's probably not in as good a shape now as she was then. Chad and my son were good swimmers, too, but that was several years ago."

Kennedy sighed. "Sounds like my sister's just up to her old tricks again. She has to be the center of attention everywhere she goes."

"She certainly got Chad's attention, too." I smiled.

"Barf," Kennedy said.

"Oh, don't hate on your sister." I borrowed that expression from my great-grandson, Cameron.

"I'm not hating on her."

I winked at her. "That's what all haters say. But I'll give you the benefit of the doubt, seeing as you're about to start the next chapter in your own love story in just a few days."

Kennedy took a sip of her wine.

"Aren't you ecstatic?" I asked.

"Very," she said very dryly.

Gary started drinkin' too.

The way they was acting, you'd think this was one of them arranged marriages or a situation where somebody needed a pass into America.

We ate mostly in silence until Frank changed the subject. "What's next on the itinerary?"

"A visit to the gardens today this morning," Kennedy said to my husband. "For my maids of honor, a trip to the salon later today."

"Oh, that'll be nice. Did you get a chance to ask Whitney about rejoining the wedding?"

Kennedy's face went extra-sour. "I did. She said absolutely not."

"Hmm. That's odd. When I spoke to Whitney, she said you never even talked to her about it."

Kennedy wiped her mouth with a linen napkin. "Mama B, I didn't want to tell you this. But there's something you should know about Whitney. She's a liar. A pathological liar. She lies about everything and everyone, including herself."

Now, back in my day, calling somebody a liar was

fightin' words. People took pride in their honesty. So I don't take being lied to lightly. Problem was, I couldn't tell which sister to believe at the moment 'cause Kennedy had two sides to her, too.

Here come the dip-seven-times twins into the dining area. Kennedy waved them over. Instantly, her face strapped on a fake, beauty pageant smile. I realized then, this girl was busy playing a role for everybody. The last thing she needed was to add "fake wife" to the cast of characters in her life.

"Hey! Get some chairs. We'll scoot over," Kennedy said to them.

Jordan and River pulled two chairs to either side of the table. So now, it was me and Frank on the north side. Gary and Kennedy on the south side. And the twins sitting on the east and west. Common sense should have told them to get their own table—wasn't hardly even no room on the surface for their plates.

"Jordan. River. You remember Frank and Beatrice?" Gary reintroduced us politely.

"Yes," one of them said. "Nice to see you two again."

"Are you enjoying yourselves?" The other one said real slow and loud, like me and Frank was half senile.

"We're not deaf," I said. "And yes, we're having a wonderful time."

"Oh. I'm sorry," the twin said. "I only wanted to make sure to speak clearly."

I had plenty more I could have said to her, but wasn't no need in me adding gas to the fire.

'Bout this time I wasn't even mad at Kennedy or the twins no more. I was thinking to myself, "Why on earth is Gary marryin' this gal? What's wrong with him, sittin' here actin' like this child got any business being anybody's wife?"

"I guess we'll see you on the way to the gardens, Gary," I said, standing.

"Sure thing," Gary said.

Soon as me and Frank was off the dining room tile and out of their view, I stopped and looked him straight in the face. "It's something wrong with Gary."

"Now, B—"

"Don't 'now B' me, Frank. Listen. Him and Kennedy ain't bit mo' together than a cat and a cow. Somethin' ain't right with this whole entire wedding and you know it. You can't sit up here and tell me you don't."

Frank crushed his lips together and looked away from me. "Who Gary chooses to marry is none of my business."

"You got to talk to him or something. Ain't you his friend?"

"I'm his *colleague*," Frank said.

"Well, since he thought enough of you to ask you to be in his wedding, you must be the closest thing to a friend he got. And part of your role as a semi-friend is to make sure his head is clear. He might be *on* something. Might be still depressed from his divorce. Anything! You gotta talk to him. Find out what's going on in his head."

"B—"

"I'm serious, Frank." I tapped his chest with my index finger. "This is ridiculous. Got two sisters fightin' like Mary and Martha. Bride and groom ain't hardly talkin', and every time her friends come around, she go into Miss America mode. I didn't come here for all this mess. If I wanted some drama, I could have stayed at home and argued with Son about the house instead."

"Well, maybe we should have stayed at home, B. You've done nothing but fuss and complain the whole time we've been here," Frank quipped.

"I beg your pardon. I most certainly have not."

"Might as well. This ain't your wedding. These people ain't your problem. Them two sisters probably been fightin' for years and whatever happens between Gary and Kennedy is their business. Why can't you leave them be and just enjoy this time at the beach?"

"Because I actually *care* about people, all right?" I huffed.

"B, I don't say much when you want to help out a family member or even go the extra mile for a total stranger, but now you're bringing your problem-solving skills to my friends and it's not necessary."

I didn't know whether to be mad or hurt or indignant. "I get in other people's problems because I want to help."

"Well, some people might call that being nosy," Frank said.

"*Some* people knew this about me when they married me. *Some* people need to realize this is one thing that ain't gonna change about me, so *some* people need to get over it and let *me* be *me!*"

Frank took a deep breath and spoke calmly. "I'm only asking you to stop trying to control everybody."

"And I'm asking you to stop tryna control me." I pressed all ten fingers to my chest.

Me and Frank stood there caught in a staring match. My heart rate was pumpin' while his temples was pulsin'.

"Is everything okay?" Larissa, the wedding coordinator, asked as she touched my shoulder.

"We fine," I assured her sternly.

Frank added, "We *will* be if someone relaxes."

"I am relaxed!"

"I see," Larissa said. "I'd hate to see you when you really get upset."

She was really pushing it. And so was my husband. This whole entire trip was turning out to be a bad idea and I was ready to go home. Pronto.

11

_____

Now that me and Frank had had a falling out, I didn't really have nobody to talk to except the Lord. Turns out that was exactly Who I needed to talk to. As much as I wanted to enjoy seeing God's creation in bloom in a different part of the country, my mind just wasn't right. All I could do was keep my mouth closed so I wouldn't ruin the garden trip for everyone else with my sour mood. Frank held my hand as we toured, but in my heart, I wanted to put my hands in the front pockets of my cropped pants.

As the garden guide explained to us the various species of flowers, I replayed my argument with Frank in my head. *Maybe Frank is right about my attitude.* Mind you, this wasn't the first time in my seventy-something years somebody had told me about myself. Sometimes personalities clash and ideals differ on account of the fact wasn't none of us made exactly the same and no two people live the exact same experience on Earth. Never have and never will.

I remember one time me and a lady who worked in my beauty shop named Marveline couldn't hardly agree on nothin'. We would be sitting right there in the shop seeing and hearing the exact same things, but we would have two different interpretations of what happened.

Like this one time, a would-be customer came into the shop and asked, "Y'all do braiding?"

I was just about to answer, "No, we don't have nobody here to do braiding." And I was gonna tell her where she could get some braiding done.

But Marveline beat me. She blurted out, "You see us sittin' here pressin' and permin' hair. Do it look like we do braidin' to you?"

And the woman turned around and walked right out the shop.

"Marveline! Why you get all feisty with her!" I fussed. That's all my mouth said, but my eyes was pointin' at the patrons we already had in the store 'cause it's downright unprofessional to be so mean in front of customers.

"B, that woman know good and well we don't do braids. She just came in here to make fun of us and let us know we behind the times. She was tryna be funny!"

"Now, why couldn't she just be somebody new in town asking about our services. I ain't never seen her before. You?"

Marveline popped her gum. "Naw, I ain't never seen her, but I know how to see through people's games. You the only one around here who can't figure out what's *really* going on. Maybe if you'd take your head out the Bible, you could see the world for what it really is."

That was back when I was still smart-mouthed, so I ain't gonna tell you what I said back to Marveline, 'cause I don't use them kind of words no more.

There was also a man who used to go to Mt. Zion a long time ago named Brother Bosco. Now, it was early in 1970 and a lot of us in the black community was and always had been suspicious of white folk. President Kennedy had been assassinated, and Lord knows his death set the idea of racial harmony back about fifteen years. Dr. King hadn't quite been dead two years at that point, I don't think.

Anyhow, Brother Bosco got it in his mind that we didn't need no white folk coming to our church for no reason whatsoever. This was before Peasner had its own food pantry for people to come get help. Mt. Zion used to hand out free meals a few days a week in the summer since so many of the city's kids would go without meals, with school being out and everything. Brother Bosco suggested we shouldn't serve the little hungry white families because, according to him, them churches on the other side of the tracks probably wouldn't have served us had we showed up on the steps of First Baptist.

"We gotta learn to take care of our own," he had fussed during the hospitality meeting which, as I recall, no one had actually invited him to seeing as the ink hadn't even dried on his church membership card.

"Do you propose we turn them away?" I asked.

"No. Just put up a blacks-only sign, the same way they did us. They'll get the message and stop coming altogether," he smirked.

Pastor Phillips had fixed his lips to intervene, I'm sure, but I had to get to the bottom of Brother Bosco's two-second thought process. "A blacks-only sign, huh?"

Brother Bosco nodded. "Give them a taste of their own medicine. It's the only way they gon' understand —they need us more than we need them! We built this country!"

Pastor Phillips started, "Well, here at—"

"And you think the best way to make things right is to refuse to feed hungry children because God created them white?" I asked, cutting off Pastor Phillips.

"Might not be the *best* way, but it's a way! Like I

said, you gotta give people a taste of their own medicine."

I slid my Bible across the table, straight over to him. "Show me that in the Word."

He flipped through like he was going to actually find such a Scripture that says we called to return evil for evil. And we all sat there waiting while his little finger went up and down some pages. I mean, his lips was just-a movin' like he was gonna really find it.

"Why don't you check the book of Revelation," I suggested for no good reason.

Chile, he flipped to the *front* of the Bible, over there whispering, "Revelationsssss, Revelationsssr."

"It don't have no 's' on the end," I barked.

I avoided looking up at Pastor because I knew he would have given me an eye to stop this interrogation.

Well, Brother Bosco stopped about halfway through the Bible and sat back. "I can't find it right now, but I still say you gotta treat people exactly the way they *deserve* to be treated."

"Is that how Jesus treats you all the time—exactly the way you deserve?" I asked him point blank.

Brother Bosco shuffled in his chair. "Naw, not always."

"Then I'mma need you to be quiet about this here food program. We gon' feed every child who come through that door—red, yellow, green, brown, or striped!"

Well, I know I was right with what I told Brother Bosco, but he stopped coming to church after that and Pastor Phillips and Geneva had a talk with me about it. Said I was coming down too hard on the man. They wanted me to simmer down a bit and don't cut the pastor off no more when he's trying to talk.

I did repent for over talking my pastor, but I couldn't agree with them about how Brother Bosco needed to be handled and I sure wasn't about to search to and fro to find him and bring him back to Mt. Zion. People like him—trying to fight hate with hate—they just don't understand: You ain't gonna never win that way. Pastor told me I was doing the same thing as Brother Bosco by gettin' so mad and bein' disrespectful to him.

We had to agree to disagree.

All of that to say I ain't no stranger to criticism. I done had disagreements with peoples before, even my beloved pastor. But coming from Frank, though, at this stage in my walk with God—it rattled me. Despite my reaction in the dining hall, I respect my husband and what he says. He's a wise man of God and he has taught me a lot about God's love and grace over the time we been together. He even got me to going to a multi-cultural church, which I really didn't think I was cut out for. But when we be in Frank's church and all them different colored hands be raised toward heaven praising the Lord, it's a beautiful sight to see.

Make you wonder why we all divided up on Sunday morning in the first place.

Anyhow, Frank kept holding my hand through the whole garden tour. It was beautiful, indeed, and I should have been happy, but I wasn't. Didn't stop him from treating me like his wife, though, and it almost made me mad because I kind of wished he had an attitude, too, then I wouldn't be the only one actin' up.

Frank and the men wanted to go get a drink when we returned from the gardens. He kissed me on the cheek as I boarded the elevator to return to our room.

"I love you, B."

"Mmmm hmmm. You, too," was as close as I could get to a gracious reply.

As I entered our hotel room, thinking about what a blessing Frank had been to me, tears came to my eyes. This was supposed to be a good trip. A time to kick our feet up. All we'd managed to kick up was a whirlwind of fussin'. Right up until that very moment, I had been thinking the reason I was experiencing so much strife on this trip was because that match up of Gary and Kennedy was all wrong; if they was meant to be, things would have gone smoother.

But when me and Frank ain't on one accord—which we really hadn't been since Son called my cell phone—something else is going on. In my spirit, I heard clear as a bell: *You* might be on vacation, but the enemy ain't.

"Lord Jesus, do that rascal ever take a break?" I whispered.

Well, I really didn't need an answer 'cause it was already clear to me. If my adversary didn't take a vacation, I didn't need to take one either. I set my purse on the chair and opened up the front part of my suitcase, where I had packed my Bible and journal. I had stuffed them into place hastily in the last minute double-check before we flew out. They had been sitting in that front compartment, untouched since the night before I got on the plane.

I carried myself and my portable "quiet time station" to the dining area and spread my materials out on the table.

That old flesh in me started to get riled up. Had the nerve to fuss, "You mean I can't even enjoy a vacation without the Lord?"

Ha! The way that old dead memory-voice put it made absolutely no sense. God is my best friend. How could I even enjoy myself without Him on the trip? How could I call myself admiring the beauty of His creation on my vacation without hardly saying so much as "Good morning" to Him? My time alone with Him every day wasn't a burden—it was a privilege and a necessity. Just like brushing my teeth. Ain't a day go by—rain, shine, sleet, snow, sick, well, a funeral, a baby shower, a trip out of town—don't matter, I still brush my teeth *every* morning, first thing. I don't even think about not doing it 'cause that would make for an unpleasant sensation in my mouth all day.

Well, obviously neglecting my time with Him was putting an unpleasant sensation in my life. But when I thought about it some more, I rolled my eyes. That's how the devil do. He like to wait till you get busy or distracted and then he strike. That's why the Bible says he like a lion. Lions don't do no loud roarin' when they lookin' for prey. They got to sneak up on animals when they drinkin' water or playin' around in the mud. And they go after the slowest one in the pack, the weakest one in the most vulnerable position on that particular day.

Yep, that's just how the enemy is. He waited until he knew good and well I hadn't gotten my rest because of the flooding in the house, until I was offended by the wedding, until my schedule was full, until I was feeling a little guilty about the situation with Son and Frank...all that added with me being out of my normal routine of prayer. It was a perfect time to strike.

"You had your fun, Satan, but it stops now," I said out loud as I opened my Bible to the fifteenth book of Proverbs, coinciding with the day's date. Honey, me and the Lord had a good time as I meditated on His words about *my* words. Wisdom, good words, and a good heart were all mine in Christ Jesus, and I needed to claim them whether I was in Texas or Timbuktu. I already knew this truth, of course, but I had lost sight of it in the process of, well, I guess it was just life outside of my usual zone.

Oh, but what an assurance the Lord gave me that He was yet God in Florida, too. His Word was just as true here as any other place, and the Jesus in me is the same yesterday, today, and forevermore. Oooh, the sweet Holy Spirit sure do bring stuff to remembrance, just like Jesus promised He would!

I spent my time talking to the One who made all those beautiful flowers I'd just seen. He accepted my apology for leaving Him out of my trip. I had to *re*-repent for my attitude about Gary and Kennedy, and I set in my heart to apologize to Frank the moment I saw him. Even though I wasn't entirely wrong by what I said, my words that came out of my mouth wouldn't have been so nasty if I had "brushed my teeth" in the spiritual sense that morning.

It's a good thing when you got a forgiving spouse 'cause you sho' gonna need forgiveness over and over again!

12

Next on the day's agenda was for the wedding party gals to go get their nails and feet done. Well, I wasn't in the wedding, but my feet was sure in need of a good paraffin wax, so I called Larissa at the number she had provided on the itinerary to see if I could join them.

"No problem," she said.

"Thank you. And I want to apologize for snapping at you earlier. I was upset about something that didn't have nothing to do with you. But I had a little come-to-Jesus meetin' and I'm all right now."

Larissa chuckled, "We all need one of those every now and then, huh?"

"Looks like I need one *every* day," I admitted. "What time should I meet up with the ladies?"

"The shuttle should arrive around two-thirty to take us to the spa."

"I'll be there with bells on."

"Great!"

My wish that Frank would come back to the hotel room before I left for the salon was granted. I wanted to greet him with a smile and an "I'm sorry" fresh on my lips. So you can imagine my surprise when I seen him walk through the door with a fresh bouquet of flowers.

He pushed his shades up on his head and came straight toward me as I came straight toward him. He held out the flowers. I took them from him.

"I'm sorry," we both said at the same time. We hugged, which set my mind in peace-mode.

"No, I'm really sorry," I insisted, looking up at him. "I had a talk with the Lord and I realize I've been distracted while we've been here. Been off my spiritual watch."

"And I've been off mine, too. You're right. If Gary considers me a friend, I should *be* a friend to him as well.."

"So, you gonna talk to him?" I asked.

"I did. At the bar."

"What did he say?"

"He said he knows Kennedy's not head-over-heels in love. He knows she's mostly looking for stability. But they're good together. Friendly, when all her friends aren't around. Gary said he's already done the head-over-heels thing once and it didn't work out. He'd like something more practical this time around. She's a good girl. A *beautiful* girl. Says his divorce alienated him from his children and he has no one. So Kennedy's as much a find for him as he is one for her."

"Stability, huh? That's what she wants from Gary? He didn't seem too stable to me. I mean, he ain't been long divorced. And when he was married, don't look like he played the stable role to me," I observed, still cuddled in Frank's embrace.

"She's looking for financial stability as well as someone who's going to be a constant in her life. She started losing her mother as a teenager, so Kennedy's been in a panic all her life. Now, with Gary, she's calm. And just so you know, Gary didn't start steppin' out on his wife until she found another beau. I can attest to that for a fact. Gary's not perfect, but he is honest. When Gary found out his wife had been unfaithful, it broke his heart. Turned him into a man he probably didn't know he could be. Mean. Nasty. Vindictive. He lashed out at everybody, including his kids. Didn't make no sense, but you know how it is when people are hurt. They take it out on the closest ones."

"So she marryin' him for stability and he marryin' her so he can keep her at a distance and not get hurt again?" I summed up.

"I wouldn't say that second part is true. He thinks she might eventually fall in love with him and vice versa."

"Really?"

"Yes. He's going for the reverse-plan, marry now, fall in love later."

"And he don't think this is gonna backfire?"

Frank looked up at the ceiling, out the patio, then back at me. "Here we are the day before the wedding. The plan is working so far. Not only that, Gary says he and Kennedy actually enjoy each other's company. It's the tension of the wedding and having her sister around and having to impress her friends that's the real problem."

I pinched the bridge of my nose, lifting my glasses up slightly.

"B, it's a free world. And you and I both know people who have married for far worse reasons than stability and companionship."

He wasn't lying about that. One of my cousins married a woman because she made the best hotwater cornbread. "I gotsta have this cornbread in my life," he had answered when my aunt asked him why on earth he would marry someone he hadn't known but six weeks.

That hotwater cornbread must have been anointed because they sure stayed married forty-something years, until he died.

"I suppose so," I had to agree.

I told Frank about my plans to go to the spa with the ladies.

He frowned up. "So you gonna leave me here by myself, huh?"

"I'll be back soon enough with nice, soft, pretty feet."

He winked at me. "Don't take all day, you hear?"

"I hear you loud and clear."

I DON'T THINK the twins was too happy about me tagging along for the wedding party trip. One of them made reference to the fact that I wasn't on the list when we arrived at the spa. The only difference between the beauty of the spa and the hotel was the spa smelled like a soothing combination of vanilla, lavender, and almond. They could have bottled up that air and sold it.

But no, one of the twins had to stink things up with a short, quippy reference to me. She thumbed toward me, "She's not supposed to be here, but she is. Can you squeeze her in?"

The receptionist looked at the appointment book and then up at the twin again. "Bea Jackson?"

I raised my finger. "Yes. That's me."

"Perfect. Larissa already informed us there would be an extra person. It's all good."

"Glad to hear it," I said with a smug grin on my face. Then I borrowed one of Frank's lines. "I'm so glad it's a free world and people can make appointments as they please."

The twins all but rolled their eyes. "I've got to go to the restroom," one of 'em said. They both headed off in the direction of the lavatory signs, which left me and Kennedy sitting on a small bench together near the reception desk.

"Mama B, I'm sorry about my friends. I think they're jealous of Gary. My friends want me all to themselves sometimes," Kennedy said. "The three of us have been stuck together like glue since we were in high school. They were the only friends I had when my mom died, and that's something I'll always be grateful for."

"Well, I ain't sayin' you shouldn't stay friends with them, but old friends should know how to treat your new friends."

Kennedy nudged me. "So we're friends now?"

I peered at her, then smiled back. "We are so long as you don't treat me no different in front of the baptism gals. I done had enough of you playin' all these roles. One way with your friends, one way with your sister, one way with your fiancé when your friends aren't around, another way when they are around. Honey, don't you get tired of trying to figure out how and when to act?"

She puckered her lips, then twisted them to the side. "Doesn't everybody have, like, different ways they act with different people? I mean, it's like knowing your audience."

"Yeah, when you up on a stage performing. But life ain't meant to be one big performance. While you doin' all this actin' for other people and tryin' to see what they want you to be to them, you need to be learnin' who *Kennedy* is. Better yet, who *God* says Kennedy is."

She opened her mouth to speak, but nothing came out. She thought again. "That's one thing I like about Gary. When it's just the two of us, I feel free. Like I can be my real self, whoever that is."

Though I was glad to hear her say something nice about her fiancé, for once, I had to ask, "You don't know who you are, baby? Your dreams, your goals, what you want to be when you grow up?"

Kennedy laughed. "No. Not really. I just...when my mom got sick, I became her caregiver and my little sister's second mom. That's who I was."

"Who were you *after* your mother died?"

"I was alone. Afraid. My dad was gone. My sister and I didn't really have anyone we could count on." She blinked rapidly. "And we were broke. My mom cashed in everything she could to pay for specialists and pharmaceuticals and treatments. Trying to stay alive."

"I'm so sorry to hear that, Kennedy."

"It's okay. I really am glad she's not suffering anymore."

People who done seen their loved ones die in anguish really do welcome the sweet rest death brings.

"I know that's right. Watchin' the folk you love suffer is hard. Real hard."

Kennedy nodded.

"But you still didn't tell me who *you* are. What you'd like to do with *your* life."

She paused. Looked down at her empty hands. "I guess I never thought about it."

"Well, it's certainly something to consider," I said. "Here you are. About to get married. If you don't know you, how you gon' give the best of this unknown 'you' to Gary?"

She grumbled to herself. "I might not know me, but I know Gary. He's truthful. And strong. He says what he means and means what he says. I like that about him. He makes me feel safe again, like before my mom died."

It occurred to me just then that Kennedy was surrounded by liars and fake people, from her sister to those twins. Everybody except Gary.

Doctors had probably given her false hope. Her own Daddy had abandoned her, which is a form of a lie. Maybe even her own mother had made promises to get well to keep from having her daughter worry. Gary was the closest thing to truth Kennedy knew, and people always gravitate toward the truth because it's the highest ground we got in this sinking world.

"Well, I'm glad for you and Gary. I truly am," I admitted to myself as much as her. God works in mysterious ways. If He wanted to reveal Himself to Kennedy through this marriage with Gary, as awkward as it appeared, I would pray for all of this to work for their good. Lord knows, both of their hearts needed mending.

"But I still want you to think about the purpose for *your* life, which has its own unique value. Let's say you're blessed to live a whole 'nother sixty-something years, till you're ninety-something years old. When you sittin' on your front porch in a rocking chair with younger family members all around you. When one of them asks you what your life was like, what do you want to be able to tell them?"

Kennedy took a deep breath. Her eyes filled with wonder. "Oh my gosh. Now that you've put it that way, I'm like...wow. Anything could happen between now and then. Sixty years is like, forever."

"Watch out now, 'cause I'm older than sixty," I warned her.

She laughed. "Okay."

"You think about it, though, 'cause them sixty years will come and go just like that." I snapped my fingers. "You don't want to fill them up with a bunch of regrets. And you sure don't want to base the next sixty on the first thirty, seeing as things didn't really go an ideal way or whatnot for the first part."

I rose to a standing position. "I'm gonna go pick out a color for my feet. You keep thinkin' on what I said."

"Yes, ma'am."

Seem like soon as I got up, my bladder told me I needed to hit the ladies' room myself. So I took a detour and slipped into the first stall. Two toilets flushed down the row and pairs of shoes flip-flopped down the aisle, toward the sink, I'm thinkin', so the ladies could wash their hands.

"I can't wait for this wedding to be over."

I recognized the voice as coming from one of the Naaman's-bathtub twins.

"I know, right? It's so crazy."

"*Kennedy's* so crazy. I mean, yeah, he's a doctor, but he's not, like, one of the *uber-rich* ones with a specialty," a twin remarked. "There's no way I'd marry that old geezer. He has *gray hair* around the edges!"

I don't know if they thought the water running in the sink would drown out their voices, if they didn't hear me when I walked into my stall, or if they just plain didn't care that someone might be listening.

They both giggled. The water stopped. I heard the paper towels rollers dispensing paper automatically.

Lord, these girls are a sad lot of friends!

"Look at the bright side. We got a free trip to Florida compliments of the president of the Jordan River fan club."

I heard them slap hands and chant, "Cha-ching!"

"It's the least she could do after all these years of letting her hang around us. She'd be a total loser without us."

Now, you know I was caught between whether to stay in my stall or come out and let them have it!

Father God! What do I do? For once on this trip, I was gonna follow the proper procedure and ask Him first. I tell you what, I sure was surprised by the stirring I felt in my spirit to go and confront the twins. He didn't have to tell me twice.

I hurried up and got out of that stall, so I could catch them in the act.

"I give them five years before they're divorced."

"Two."

"Bet."

"You're on!"

They was both giggling by the trash can when they caught my reflection in the mirror.

The one closest to me huffed. "*You.*"

"You and you!" I pointed at both of them. "How you call yourself friends with Kennedy and you standin' here talkin' about her like she got a tail on her!"

"Stay out of our business, old lady," one of them warned. "Kennedy's been our friend for a long time."

"Friend?" I asked incredulously. "Friends ain't two-faced."

The other one wrinkled her nose at me. "What does that even mean? Is this something you used to say when TV was, like, monochrome?"

They busted out laughing at the silly joke.

I could feel my flesh rising up on the inside of me. But then the Spirit took over and asked me a question: Why on earth would I let my blood pressure go up one tittle over a word comin' out of these two's mouths?

I laughed, which caught them off guard. "I feel sorry for you two. If this is the way y'all treat people, you got a whole lotta payback comin'. I don't know how you close your eyes in peace at night. I'm sure this ain't how your parents raised you. Nobody wants their beautiful twin daughters to grow up and be con-artists."

They was standin' there lookin' pitiful. Half-mad and half-hurt. Now, I wasn't intending on leaving them in that despicable state. Their smooth faces and bright eyes reminded me that I was dealin' with very young people, after all. They had time to get it right, and I knew just Who could help them do it.

"Y'all heard about Jesus?" I asked point blank.

"Um, duh! Who hasn't?"

This one, who I could now see had a little mole above her lip, seemed to always talk first.

"Well, hearin' about Him and knowing Him is two different things. Now, He loves—"

"We're soooo not here for a Sunday school lesson. We had enough of those growing up, thank you very much," the leader said. "Why don't you just leave us alone? You're not really supposed to be here at the nail salon anyway."

I took that as a sign that they wasn't ready to hear the gospel. Fine with me. Somebody had planted, I'd done my part to water. It was up to God to do the growin'.

I shrugged. "I'll leave you alone. No problem. But one day you're gonna realize the only people you got in your corner is just as miserable and unhappy as you. And the sad thing for the both of you is you look just like each other, so every time you see her"—I pointed at one—"and every time you see her"—I pointed at the other—"you gonna see your sad, sorry self all over again. When the day comes you're tired of seeing sad and sorry, God'll be waitin' on ya."

I gazed at the followin' twin, whose eyes weren't as hard and cold as her sister's. "Both of you."

Kennedy entered the restroom. "Hey! Is the party in here now?" Her grin melted as the head-twin threw a somber glance.

"Well. Miss B, here, was just telling us that she

doesn't understand why you're marrying Gary."

My mouth flew open. "I—"

"Yep," the rude one kept going, "she even said she gives your marriage five years, tops."

"I said no sucha thing—*you* said that!"

Kennedy crossed her arms and peered at me. "So you've been against me all this time?"

"I ain't the one against you. It's *these* two you need to be questioning! They're the ones claiming to be your friends when all they've ever done is use you."

The beauty-mark twin declared, "How would you know? You've known us for, what... two days now?"

"Because I've known your *type* all my life."

I returned my attention to Kennedy, who was obviously flustered and frustrated. "If you really look back over the pattern of your friendship, you'll see you been on the givin' end of things for a long time with these two."

The beauty-mark twin declared, "She's lying! She said you must be some kind of gold digger. Right, Jordan?"

Jordan swallowed.

"*Right,* Jordan?" River repeated urgently.

"Right," the softer twin mumbled regretfully.

Somehow Kennedy missed that hesitation because the next thing she said to me was, "Well, if you feel that way, you and my sister can both catch the next plane back to Dallas!"

And with that, she and the wonder twins marched out of the restroom with the twins' ponytails bouncing in sync.

Ten Mississippi. Nine Mississippi. Eight Mississippi.

Saints of the Most High God, I promise you: I had never wanted to snatch a person by the hair until that exact moment. I'd seen the damage hair-snatching could do on some of my clients, actually, when I was a beautician. And I'd seen TV shows where people talked about how they "snapped" and blacked out and did something out of they character without thinking about it.

I understood exactly what they meant that day.

Seven Mississippi. Six Mississippi. Five Mississippi.

Countin' them Mississippi's backwards wasn't really helping, so I changed my strategy.

Four Holy Ghost Help Me. Three Holy Ghost Help Me. Two Holy Ghost Help Me.

Whew! That was better. I could see straight again.

Now. I was still alone in the restroom and was regaining my wits, really tryin' to understand what had just happened. This wasn't the first time I'd been lied on. But to my face? And so viciously? And to have somebody confirm the lie, and somebody believe the lie on top of it all?

Maybe I did need to go back to Dallas after all. This was too much evil and drama for a beachfront vacation.

13

Wedding invitation or not, my feet still needed a pedicure, so I took care of my beauty treatment first, then headed back to the hotel in a cab all by myself. My husband would have been furious had he known I'd been galavantin' around Florida unescorted. What he wouldn't have understood was that anybody who messed with me that day would have picked the wrong senior citizen to cross.

I ain't the one. Not right now. My mouth didn't speak the words, but my face must have told the cab driver to turn around and be quiet when he tried to make friendly talk with me on the way back to the hotel. I gave him the address, he drove, and I gave him the money plus a tip when he dropped me off at the Rockefeller building.

Thankfully, Frank wasn't in our room when I returned. Not that I would have minded his presence. I was just glad for a moment to myself. A moment with the Lord, actually. He's the one I needed to talk to. But the red, blinking light on the phone caught my attention as I lifted the sling purse over my head and set it on the counter.

I rested on the edge of the bed and lifted the receiver while reading the phone's panel for instructions. A red, blinking light meant I had a message at the front desk. I dialed "o" and waited for someone to answer.

"Guest services. How may I help you?"

"Yes, this is Bea Jackson. My light is blinking. Do I have a message?"

He paused. "Ummm...yes. One moment here."

My teeth clenched involuntarily. Whoever left this message must have been desperate to reach me, callin' the front desk of the Rockefeller and all.

"Yes. Your daughter, Debra Kay, left a message for you to call her as soon as possible."

"Oh, Lord," escaped my lips. "Thank you." I dropped the phone back on its cradle.

Why didn't she call me on my cell?

Must have had something to do with Son. I already knew he must have told her to sidestep Frank to give me a message. But Debra Kay wasn't one to play those kinds of games with Son. Had he brain-washed her?

I rang her number and she answered right away. "Momma."

"What's going on?"

"Son."

"What now?"

"He's crazy. He's gotten a lawyer. He's trying to get all of us to sue you. He filed something with the county and, according to him, you have so many hours to respond before the courts get involved with the house. He's got Aunt Ida Mae involved, too, and she's signed all kinds of papers saying you're a slum-lord, you don't keep the house up, she questions your sanity...on and on."

"Well, you're right about one thing," I said, "Son is out of his mind at the moment."

Debra Kay continued, "I told him I wasn't signin' no papers, but I don't know what to do. I know you're on vacation and supposed to be enjoying yourself, but since time is supposedly of the essence, I had to call you. Son said you weren't answering your phone, so I left the message with the hotel."

"*Son* is the only one banned from phone calls at the moment."

"Who banned him? Frank?"

"Yes, because Son kept callin' me worryin' me about the house when he's supposed to be the landlord. Did he bother to tell you that there was a plumbing leak right before we left and me and Frank had to get up in the middle of the night to go handle it while Son stayed sound asleep in bed despite our texts?" I asked my daughter as though cross-examining her on a witness stand.

"Slow down, Momma. I'm not the enemy. Just the messenger."

I sighed. "I'm sorry. Thank you, Debra Kay. I'll handle it from here."

"What are you going to do?"

"I don't know. Well, yes I do. First I'm gonna pray. Then I'm probably gonna get a flight back to Dallas 'cause things ain't goin' too well for me here in Florida anyway."

"What's happening?"

I shook my head as though she could see me. "It's a long story. Nothing you'd want to hear."

A clicking sound came from the front door. Frank.

I rushed Debra Kay off the phone. "Thank you for calling, baby. I'll get back with you."

"Take care, Momma."

"You, too."

Frank entered just as I hung up. I announced, "Frank, I'm ready to go back home."

He stopped mid-stride. Eyes wide open. "O-kaaaay...ummm...we're here for the wedding."

"Well, I've been uninvited to the wedding by the

bride herself. And now Son has filed some kind of paperwork against me regarding the house, and I'm good and tired of this whole trip. I guess we gotta stay so you can be in the wedding, but after that, I wanna catch the first thing smokin' to Dallas."

"Wait. Back up. Uninvited to the wedding?"

How does he figure that was the most important thing I just said?

Frank sat next to me as though I needed comforting. "Kennedy asked you not to come to the wedding?"

"She *told* me not to come. Said me and Whitney could go on home if we wanted."

"And what brought that about?"

I gave him the short version of how the twins had ganged up on me in the restroom at the nail parlor. How Kennedy had believed their lies, as she had obviously been deceived for the entire life of their dead friendship.

"I'll talk to Gary. He'll talk to Kennedy. She'll let you come to the wedding."

"But I ain't got a mind to go to the wedding. What I really want to do is go home. This minute. I got bigger fish to fry."

"B, whatever papers Son *claims* he filed will be sitting under somebody's paperweight for the next few days since it's already Thursday afternoon. We'll get attorneys on it right away."

I rubbed my forehead. "I don't want to fight Son over the house. I don't want to fight him over anything, really."

Frank breathed deeply. He pulled my hand away from my forehead. Placed it in his hands. Closed his eyes. "Father God."

I closed my eyes, too. I had planned to pray, of course, but not one of these nice, calm prayers I knew Frank was about to pray to our Father. Me and God had a different way. I liked to fuss first. Get it all out, like David did in the Bible. David would put his heart —whether wrong or right—before the Lord first and tell Him how he really felt, then the Lord, in His love, brought David back to his senses. To the truth.

Frank liked to bypass the heated emotions and get straight to the truth. "Lord, You alone know the ins and outs of the heart. Of every relationship. Every friendship, every marriage, every engagement. Every parent and child. And you know the very best solution to every single problem. Lord, we call Your best into action right now. Your will be done on earth as it is in heaven right now. We cast down confusion and fear. We speak peace and understanding to the situations facing us now. Be glorified. In Jesus's name. Amen."

"Amen," I agreed sincerely. It was done. Peace swept through me, just like Frank had declared. Wasn't really no need in me re-hashin' what my husband had cast away. He was right. If God was God —*and He is*—wasn't no need in me bitin' my fingernails over something I couldn't fix that day. And wasn't no need in me getting all huffy over a wedding I never wanted to attend in the first place. Besides, the Lord gave me and Albert that house and everything in it. It was His to give, His to take away or redistribute. Maybe there was someone who needed their first house while I was livin' in my second one.

It's funny how things start clearin' up in your mind even before they clear up in reality when you give them over to God.

I flipped off my sandals, swung my legs onto Frank's lap, laid back into the mattress and grabbed the remote control.

"So...are you going to Karaoke Night with us?"

The last thing I needed was to sit up and listen to a bunch of off-key folk croaking out the lyrics to *Billie Jean*. "No. I think I'm gonna do something I haven't done in a while."

"What's that?" Frank asked, amused.

"I'm gonna lay here in this bed and watch me some TV for about two or three hours in a row."

My husband squinted his eyes. "Who are you and what have you done with my wife?"

We froze for a second, then laughed together.

"Just need to sit for a spell, that's all," I told him.

"I can't argue with that."

Frank looked down at my feet.

I wriggled my toes.

"Woman, you got the prettiest feet I've ever seen."

He began massaging my feet. Then he kissed my legs.

That's all I'm at liberty to tell you about regarding that particular afternoon of our reclaimed vacation.

FRANK DIDN'T MAKE it to the Karaoke Night, but he did go to the dinner buffet later in the evening where, according to him, he and Gary agreed that I was re-invited to attend the wedding via the groom. Gary said he'd patch things up with Kennedy, so I could come to the bachelorette party that night.

"Frank, you know I ain't got no business at a party like that with all those young girls. They liable to have a male dancer and wild drinkin' and goin's-on." I scowled, turning down the volume on the television show. "You know better than to let him think I was going to such a thing."

"One of his aunts is going," Frank carried on as though he hadn't even heard me. He took off his cotton pullover shirt and hung it in the closet. "Kennedy's face blushed when she admitted to it. But she said if you came, she wouldn't feel so bad."

"Well, she gon' be feelin' bad tonight 'cause I won't

be there. And why are you actin' like you don't know me on this here trip?"

Frank jerked his head back.

"You been springin' all kinds of stuff on me with this trip, from Kennedy's age, to asking me to be in the wedding, to all but signing me up to go witness a strippin' incident. What in the world is happening with you?"

My half-thought-out, spur-of-the-moment observation wasn't actually meant to be an accusation, but the awkward look on my husband's face told me I'd hit a raw nerve.

I turned the television off. Sat straight up in bed. "Frank Wilson, what's going on?"

14

Frank poked his lips out, like he was thinkin' hard. Too hard.

"You might as well go ahead and tell me," I prodded him.

He paced the side of the bed a few times. Hung his hand on the back of his neck.

"Spit it out," I very nearly yelled. There's a time and a place for sugar-coating. This here right now wasn't it.

Frank stopped. Stood right in front of me and looked down into my face. "Gary and I are planning to go into business together when I retire."

I raised an eyebrow. "Is that so?"

"Yes. I was really hoping you and Kennedy would hit it off since we'll probably be seeing a lot of them, with the business and all."

"What kind of business you two cookin' up? And why am I just now hearing about it?"

"Medical care for seniors. We're going to buy homes, staff them with caregivers, and provide healthy, safe, comfortable environments for the elderly. It's a very lucrative business, especially with more of the population living longer."

"Frank, *we* old. How you gonna start runnin' a home for the elderly and you on the home stretch yourself? And I repeat—why am I the last to know?"

"Actually, you're one of the first," Frank said with a big smile on his face like I was supposed to be happy about it. "We're still in the planning phase, B. Speculative, but promising. There's not a whole lot to discuss right now."

"Yes, there is. You was just complaining a few days ago that you didn't want us to have to manage two households. You was thinkin' about liquidatin' and movin' to a beach like this one here. Now you want to start a new business?"

My husband pulled the chair from the desk over to the bed and sat across from me. His eyes beamed with excitement and his face lit up as though he was about to tell me a fairytale. "B, people run businesses from remote locations all the time. And the situation with the house...it's different."

"No it ain't!" My voice filled with emotion, matching my eyes and my chest. "The business and the house—both of them are chores, things we'd have to stay on top of."

"Yes, but the house...I don't have a whole lot of influence over that situation. I can't oversee what happens there, the decisions are not mine to make. I'm an outsider, really."

"So what you're saying is you don't want to deal with my house in your old age because you don't have control over the situation?"

Frank bit his bottom lip. "Hmmm. Yeah. I think you're right," he admitted. "What can I say? I'm old school. Bottom line, it's my job to make sure you're taken care of. With the house, I can't minimize the risk, I can't make executive decisions because it's not mine. But a business, even one that requires commitment, is one that I can oversee and make sure it's an asset."

"But We. Is. Old, Frank. O.L.D." I clapped the letters for emphasis, leaning in toward him.

"Not too old to contribute to society. Listen, the only reason I haven't retired before now is because I know too many people who retire and they go downhill from there. Their bodies go, their minds go—when you lose your purpose for living, that's the beginning of the end."

I shook my head. "Naw, I can't agree 'cause that ain't what happened to me. I ain't got no day job, but my life is plenty busy, plenty full of purpose. And I thought when you retired, we'd travel and volunteer more. That was *my* idea of retirement with you."

"We can still travel," Frank said.

"Honey, no offense, but you ain't never ran no business. You gotta be married to that thang for at least three or four years to get it off the ground. I'll be comin' up on eighty before I get you back to myself again," I fussed.

Back in my salon days, I was a witness to long hours and long nights of staying up late to balance the books, marketing, following up on bad checks, reading through new regulations, firing folks, hiring folks, folks taking money out the cash register—it was a job on top of another job.

"You'll be glad to know this is not a long-term commitment. We're going to sell the business as soon as we can," Frank informed me. "Probably to some other doctors. It'll be a nice chunk of change. A group of nurses we worked with did the same about five years ago. Once they got their business running smooth and profitable, they sold it for six million to a healthcare company."

I opened my lips to speak, but Frank cut me off with, "Big companies buy out smaller ones every day, B. Home healthcare is lucrative. Insurance companies will do anything to keep people out of nursing homes and hospitals."

Six million dollars is a whole lotta money. But the

older you get, the less all them zeroes mean to you. Time is worth far more than money, and I wasn't willing to trade money for Frank.

I crossed my arms. "So that's why you tryin' to keep on Gary's good side?" I heard the judgmental tone in my voice, but I couldn't hardly help it. The Frank I knew didn't play these kinds of games with people. He was excellent at separating business from friendship. To me, it shouldn't have mattered if I attended the wedding or not, if I liked Kennedy or not. What Frank and Gary had between them was business and expertise. I needed them to leave me out of it.

"Aside from the fact I won't actually have much access to you in a few years, what does this have to do with me? With Kennedy?"

Frank shrugged, but not like he didn't know the answer. He shrugged like he had a lot to say, but he wanted to make me feel like he was just now thinkin' through things when, I'da bet, him and Gary had already made a list of things-to-do for me and Kennedy.

"We might need you or Kennedy to plan a company outing. Help us scout homes. I mean, you can be involved as little or as much as you'd like." He took a deep breath. "I guess...I assumed that if I had a business, you'd be supportive. And if I had a business partner, my wife and I would be cordial with him and his wife. You don't have to be her best friend, but we can't have hostility at the Christmas parties. I don't need Kennedy feeding Gary lies about you. That kind of stuff eats at a person. We don't need that on our minds. It takes a lot of trust to run a business partnership."

"Well, it takes a lot of trust to run a marriage, too, and I don't appreciate you making business plans without so much as giving me a chance to decide whether or not I wanna be the CEO's wife."

"Okay. I apologize. But B, you know I don't like to come to you until I have a solution in place. I don't want to tell you half the story, get you all riled up for nothing."

"So...you knew I wouldn't like the idea?"

"I suspected you might not like to hear about our trial-and-error thinking, which is why I didn't want to talk about it until I had all my ducks in a row. But now that you done got yourself ejected from the guest list..." he offered a chuckle.

I, for one, didn't see nothin' funny. Frank was wrong. Period. He didn't have no business makin' no plans with Gary under no circumstances without talking to me first. "We ain't gonna come to no agreement on this, Frank. Not tonight. I feel like you been hidin' stuff from me. Important stuff that affects my future." I stopped just short of telling him that I didn't marry him to get neglected. And my life was perfectly fine and fulfilled before I married him—I didn't need the stress of him buildin' a business from the ground up, which he knew absolutely nothing about.

See, all Frank's life had been cut-and-dried. Get an education, get a job, do your job well and you'll get a paycheck and live life in peace. Aside from all the time it takes to run a business, there's the emotional ups-and-downs, too. What if this plan didn't work out? What if no one wanted to buy the business? What if something happened to Frank and I ended up havin' to fight with Gary and Kennedy for Frank's share of the business? This whole situation had "headache" written all over it.

Now I had to translate my thoughts to my husband in a way that didn't make him feel silly. *Help, Lord, 'cause You know this don't make a lick of sense.* "Honey, I can appreciate you wanting to get your ideas together before you come to me. But lettin' me in this late in the game is like invitin' me to attend a church, then when I get there I find out you're the pastor, which makes me the first lady, plus you signed me up to teach Sunday school classes."

"Would you still do it?" Frank asked.

"Well, in that case, yes, I would 'cause that would be God's calling on your life," I said.

"Now, you know I've already been talking to the Lord about this, right? Don't you think providing quality care for seniors is a calling, too?"

Truth be told, I done seen all kind of pitiful places people end up when their money runs out and their relatives stop checkin' on 'em. Some of them places I wouldn't take a wood rat to because it would be too nasty for the rat.

I sighed. "So this is the real reason you brought me here. To make nice with your business partner."

"B, first of all, you already *are* nice. You don't have to make or fake anything. Second, Gary is getting married tomorrow. He is a pleasant acquaintance of mine, and I'm glad to wish him well," Frank said.

Okay, I'd had enough with all this sugar-coating. *I tried, Lord. I really did.*

I opened my mouth to speak, but a check from the Holy Spirit caused me to clamp my lips together hard. It wasn't no exact phrase that He spoke to me, I just knew deep down in my knower that I didn't need to say one word. The Lord would handle it.

That's when the trusting came in.

"Well, Frank, I already done spoke my peace. Since you have prayed about it, I'm going to leave it between you and the Lord."

"Thank you. I really appreciate you believing in me. And, again, I'm sorry for blindsiding you with this. I wasn't trying to be sneaky or deceptive or play political games between you and Gary. Besides, you and I don't need an excuse to treat people right or go the extra mile. It's what we do."

Well, it still wasn't sitting right in my spirit, but it was in His hands now.

Good thing was now I knew why my husband was really trying to make sure me and Kennedy hit it off. He wanted to stay in good connections with Gary. All so he could secure our future more, financially speaking. That whole scene didn't sit well with me, but at least I wasn't in the dark anymore.

Frank got up and ran some shower water as though we hadn't just come up against a huge hurdle in our marriage. I suppose every marriage—every *real* relationship—hits it at some point. It's the point where the enemy comes in and tries to fill your mind with bad thoughts about the other person, makes you dream up wild and evil motives for them, makes you wonder if your marriage can even survive. Makes you jump to the conclusion, "I just don't like him no mo'."

I know it sounds ridiculous. There was no reason on earth for me to doubt that our marriage would fall apart whether he started the business or not. But that don't stop the enemy from suggesting the worst every chance he gets.

Of course, all of this got me to talkin' to the Lord when Frank went to take a shower. As much as I wanted to shoot down Frank's idea, I didn't see a way to shoot it down without shooting *him* down.

That's when I heard this question inside me: *Why are you shooting?*

If it was any other person telling me they were going to start something new at that age, I would have encouraged them. I woulda said, "Oh, yeah! You go right ahead! You're never too old! People need our life experience!"

But I couldn't say this to Frank because...well, because I didn't want to lose him for myself. I wanted Frank Wilson for me, not for a business with Gary, not even to provide a place for people who could no longer stay in their homes for whatever reason.

No. I wanted Frank for me, me, and more me. And the fact that he was planning to marry his business for the next five years hurt deep down in my gut 'cause this wasn't what I signed up for when I said "I do" in my golden years.

Am I wrong, Lord?

15

Whitney was on the news that Thursday night. The story played once on the ten o'clock news and again at eleven. Frank had fallen asleep before the second airing, tired from the excursions and constant interaction with Gary and friends. Made me no difference. He could sleep through the wedding, for all I cared, so long as we were on time at the airport Sunday morning for our flight.

I got up early Friday and spent some with the Lord. Just talking. I told Him I didn't know what else to think of the business idea. Wasn't really nothing left for me to say. There's one thing I understand for sure: When a real man makes up his mind to do something, nobody else's words don't mean nothin'. That's just something God put in men, I guess. It takes another well-respected man or God Himself to intervene at that point and change things around.

Frank could be about as stubborn as Son. In the entire time I have raised and known Son, he ain't never actually been wrong about anything, let him tell it. When he had that affair on Wanda and got his mistress pregnant with my granddaughter, Nikki, he still had his "reasons" for why it all happened. And then he had his "reasons" for not having a relationship with Nikki. Said he wanted to save his marriage —the same one he nearly destroyed by finding companionship in the arms of another woman. I know he's my child, but wrong is wrong. If he would have ever just come out and said when he's been wrong or made a bad choice, things would be different in my heart.

The Lord reminded me,, in that instant, not to replay all of Son's faults. He was a human being, after all. The Bible says in Psalm 103:14 that the Lord remembers how weak we are. He ought to know, seein' as He made us. It did my soul good to remember that Son was only a man.

He still needed to admit when he was wrong, though, elsewise he was going to keep up this act of being "the man" when, in actuality, there ain't no such thing as a real man who don't lean on God.

I felt the need for a drink of cold water, so I grabbed the ice bucket and my room key, slid into my house shoes, and slipped a robe over my gown. I journeyed halfway down the hall and filled the bucket with ice. Just as I was about to leave, in came Chad and Whitney. Dressed in the same hotel robe I was wearing. Both of them had wet hair and smelled of *Irish Spring.*

Lord, what is these two up to? I already knew the answer, of course. These two hadn't known each other a good week and was already sharing a bar of soap.

"Oh, hey! You up early, too?" Whitney asked. She chucked quarters into the vending machine.

"Just needed some water and ice."

She gushed, "Did you see us on the news?"

"Yes," I half-answered, still taking in the situation.

Whitney pressed a button and a candy bar dropped down from its rack in the vending machine. She reached inside and got the snack.

"People have said a lot of really nice things about you in the comments online," Chad informed me. "You should check out the network's webpage."

"Uh huh." I jiggled my ice as Chad took his turn getting candy.

When his bag of sweets tumbled down to the receptacle, he retrieved it and tore open the package immediately. "See you later, ma'am."

He and Whitney turned to walk out of the refreshment area.

"Uh hum. Um...Whitney, may I have a word with you?"

"Sure," she said, her eyes sparkling. Her tone was so innocent, so unsuspecting that I realized she saw nothing wrong with the situation. To her this whole encounter was the same as me runnin' into her and Chad at an ice cream store. No big deal.

Chad said, "I'll be back at the room."

She nodded.

He took off.

Lord, what do I say to this baby? I had to remember that I was talking to a girl who was born and raised in an age when women were being told to celebrate their sexuality, married or not. A day and time when women were expected to be "liberated" from the old way of falling in love, getting married, and then being intimate. They didn't have no social pressure to stay pure, no reputation to protect, no norms to adhere to.

Besides all that, Whitney's biggest problem wasn't that she was most likely sleepin' with a boy she just met. Whitney was crying out for attention. Help. And she'd take it from whoever would give it to her—whether it meant planning an allergic attack, pretending to drown to draw attention to herself, or sharing the most private parts of her body with a practical stranger.

"What's up, Mama B?" Whitney ripped off an inch of her chocolate bar and chewed.

"Whitney. Sweetheart."

She stopped chewing and swallowed quickly, forcefully. She covered her mouth with her hand as her eyes bugged. "What's wrong?"

You really don't want me to go down the list.

"Is my sister okay?"

"Yes. She is," I assured her, glad to know she hadn't lost all sense.

Whitney's eyes returned to normal, though she didn't express her relief verbally.

"Honey child, do you know how precious you are? How valuable you are in the Lord's eyes?"

"Ummm...yeah. I guess so? What does that have to do with anything?"

"It has to do with everything that's happened with you on this trip. Now, I know you've been lying to me."

"What are you talking about?"

"You knew you couldn't drink milk, but you knowingly ate the milk-cake and had a reaction. You said you didn't like water, but then you dove into the entire Atlantic Ocean with a boy you just met. Your stories ain't addin' up, sugar."

Whitney's mouth flopped open. Then she closed it as her eyelids became slits. "You've been talking to my sister, haven't you?"

"No. I'm talking to *you* right now about what I have personally observed. Now, looka here. You gotta stop all this lyin' to everybody. And mostly to yourself.

Else you gon' look up one day and not have a clue what the real truth is."

Looked like she was still trying to come up with some words to tell me off, but she hadn't had enough time to think of them. I could have gone on and on about how she ain't had no business with that boy and no business acting like she in distress so she could get attention all the time, but the shine in her eyes said she'd heard enough; she didn't need me to point out no more bad qualities. She had her own mirror to see her faults.

I went heavy on the encouragement side. "You told me a lot of good stuff about your momma. How she was fun, smart. How she used to watch Good Times and old TV shows, how she was a believer. That's what strong parents do. They leave their kids with a lot of fond memories. I'm sure your momma also left you with some good words about yourself that you done forgot about up until now, but I'm gonna remind you of them. You a smart girl, Whitney. *Real* smart. And pretty, too. And the Lord loves you somethin' fierce. He made you like nobody else. And when He gave you life, He gave *you* a life all your own. Your life wasn't your mother's. It ain't your sister's. It ain't mine. It's *yours*. You ain't got to try to make everybody look at you all the time 'cause you already somebody special whether we lookin' at you or not, you hear?"

The nodding of her head sent a stream of tears

down her bright red cheeks. I could just imagine how it must have torn her apart to watch her mother's demise at such an early age. Sent the poor child lookin' for attention and love through all the wrong means.

"You still loved, honey," I said to her. "You *still* loved." I pulled her into a hug. Let her cry on my shoulder. "That's right. Let it all go." We stood there for a while, her sobbing into my robe and me patting her back.

"Kennedy. She...she had mom...longer than I did," Whitney managed to say through huffs and puffs. "It's not fair. She had her longer."

"You're right. It's not. Some people get to have their mommas for seventy and eighty years. Some at least until they grow up. Some only a few years. Either way, ain't too much more in life that cut your heart as deep as losin' your momma."

Whitney sniffed. She looked up at me and asked, "Is there anything *else* in life that hurts like this, Mama B, because I won't do it, whatever it is!"

I thought about her question. "Hmph. Dying is a part of living. I done lost both my parents. My first husband. My sister. Friends. People say losing a child is the worst. Thank God, I don't know that for myself, but plenty people do. God didn't promise us a life without pain, you know. But He did promise to never leave us nor forsake us through it all."

Whitney pulled away and wiped her eyes. "I used to talk to God. I asked Him to save my mom. When He didn't, I just decided I hadn't been good enough. You know—like Santa Claus. People say if you're not good throughout the year, you won't get what you want for Christmas."

She reminded me of when I talked to my great-grandson, Cameron about God. He had a lot of unlearning about the Father to do. Apparently, so did Whitney.

"Honey, God ain't nothin' like nobody you know. And life don't usually turn out anything like what you thought it would be. Not necessarily because you bad or good. Life is *life*. It's gon' be some cold, hard days and some warm, sunny days. Either way, you put your trust in Him and when you get closer to the end, like me, you'll look back and see some of them days that felt so cold was actually kind of warm, you just didn't realize it at the time."

Whitney blubbered out, "My life is terrible."

"Whatchu gon' do 'bout it?"

She slapped her hands together. "Make it better!"

"And how you plan on doin' that?"

She sighed, her face deflated with reality. "I'm clueless."

I smiled at her. "I'm so glad you realize you can't do nothing by yourself. It takes folks thirty and forty years to get to that point sometimes. But you got it easy 'cause you already there now, thank God. Now you can get to know Him real good. Get all kind of help, all kind of wisdom when you need it. Whitney, you further along in life than you think."

"Really?" She wiped her eyes.

"Yes, ma'am. You got humility, and humility will get you all kind of favor with God."

Whitney was staring at me wide-eyed and in amazement. I done seen that look before, when the Lord turns on somebody's light from inside their heart. So beautiful to behold.

"Now, I know you said you done been to church growing up, right?"

"Yes, but I really didn't understand it all...not like I can understand you now, which is, like, totally freaking me out." She made a bewildered expression, which reminded me of one of Jesus's parables about how the enemy comes to steal the Word as soon as it's planted.

"You ain't confused, Whitney," I spoke over her. "The Lord has opened your ears to hear and your eyes to see the gospel of Christ. That will not be taken from you."

I was puttin' the enemy on notice at the same time.

"God loved you so much that He sent Christ to pay the penalty for all your sins, Whitney. You believe that?"

"Yes. I do. I don't know everything about what happened, but I do believe it."

"Whitney, them the most important words you'll ever say in your whole life. Everything else is just a matter of living life in Him. You got a constant companion from now on, my friend. You'll never be alone again, and you ain't never got to measure out what's fair, what ain't fair, who's paying you attention and who ain't. His love will fill up your heart so, you'll have a peace the world can't take away."

She nodded.

"I want you to start going to church again so you can learn more about His love for you."

"What about the other stuff?"

"What other stuff?"

She shrugged. "There are rules, right?"

"I'll let you in on a little secret, chile. The stuff He wants you to do only seems like rules when you don't know His love first. It's kind of like when you're a kid and your momma used to tell you to go to bed at a certain time. Back then, that rule seemed terrible, like your momma was cutting off the fun from your life. But later, you come to figure out she only said that to make sure you had enough rest to grow up strong. It was for your good all along, because she loved you."

"I don't know if I can do this," she said, pinching her eyebrows together.

"You can't," I agreed with her. "You gotta depend

on Him." I pointed upward. "Just like He taught your heart the truth today, He will continue to write on your heart. Just open up to Him. Talk to Him. Get to know Him like you would a friend. Like I said, church will help you read His Words."

"But what if church is boring?"

"The Bible says you a new creature now. You just go. Ask God to do the rest. Now, if you start going to a church and you ain't learnin' nothing about the Bible or God or Jesus, then you gotta find you another church. Most churches is good, but it's some out there you need to steer away from. You can call me if you need help finding a church. In fact, you can call me if you need anything."

"Wow." Whitney's eyes glazed over again. "The last time anyone said that to me was when my mom died. Everyone was telling us they would be there for us. And they were. At first. Then it was like life went on. Except I was stuck."

"Well, that's understandable. But it's time for you to get unstuck. To grow up and become the wonderful young lady the Lord created you to be. You ready?"

"Yes!" Whitney shouted.

"Ummm...hello," Chad said as he entered the ice-and-vending-turned-sanctuary space. "You coming back?"

Whitney stepped away from me to face him. "No. I've had a change."

My heart leapt inside me. I knew from the very first night of our vacation that I liked this gal.

"Okaaay," slid out of a confused Chad. "So we're not together anymore?"

Together? Was that the new word for it now? I thought they were calling it a "hook-up" or "friends with benefits". I can't keep up with how these young folk classify relationships. Back in my day, we only had two categories: married and not married. They got too much stuff in between nowadays, if you ask me.

Anyhow, Whitney asked Chad to let her back in the room, so she could get her clothes. He agreed and walked on down the hallway, still scratching his head.

Whitney gave me a thumbs-up. "I gotta start somewhere, huh?"

"I suppose so," I thumbed back. "I know the Lord will bless you for honoring what He says about your body, sweetheart."

She took off down the way nearly skipping with the joy of the Lord.

I prayed right then and there that the Lord would make Himself known to Whitney in a way that made up for all her hurts and pains and even changed her so until her relationship with Kennedy would be restored. If her mother was here, I'm sure she would want the same. But she was gone on, so it's up to the saints who are left on earth to intervene for one another's children. We gotta remember that everybody, even your worst enemy, is somebody's child and in need of prayer.

I told Frank all about what happened with me and Whitney. We both sat up in bed and laughed, thanking God because in the midst of all this confusion on the trip, He had managed to call one of His own back to His heart.

It made for a real good Friday in Miami. Me and Frank ate at the barbeque feast later than night, just smiling at one another, having our own secret celebration.

16

The morning of the wedding, I expected we would get up early again, but not nearly as early as the phone call that woke us up. The sun hadn't even peeked out yet, and already it was somebody trying to get hold of us.

Frank answered the phone. "Yes...okay. Thank you."

He put the phone back on the cradle and lay back on the pillow. "They got a package for you. Need your signature for the delivery."

I didn't even have to ask what this was all about. I knew before I showed my ID and signed my name on the 'x' it was from Son or his attorneys. "Thank you," I told the attendant as he handed me the legal-size envelope.

I took a seat in the lobby and ripped through the

ridiculous package. The letter wasn't nothing but what Debra Kay had already done told me. Filled with a bunch of empty threats like "We intend to..." and "Please be advised..." and "Contact us immediately..." Wasn't one single Latin word on the whole page, so I knew it wasn't no real legal motions taking place thus far. Any old bill collector could have written that thing. It was a shame Son had spent extra money he probably didn't have to send it through a fancy courier on a Saturday.

Soon as I finished reading that foolishness, I started dialing Son's office number. He worked a lot of Saturdays, too, for some odd reason. Them folk at his job was trying to have 24-hour customer service, I guess.

Against what Frank wanted me to do, I had snuck my cell phone out the room with me 'cause I needed to give Son a piece of my mind on *this* day that the Lord hath made.

"Hello?" he answered calmly.

"You just intent on spoilin' my vacation, ain't you?"

"Momma, this is not about you. It's business."

"If it was just business, you could wait until I get back home. But naw, you call yourself tryin' to intimidate me by overnightin' these papers in this fancy lawyer envelope, but I tell you one thing, I ain't scared of you, Son."

"We need to make a reasonable agreement.

Momma, I don't want to have to take you to court, but I will if I have to. For Daddy's sake."

I chuckled. "You really think your daddy would want you to sue me over the house?"

"My father built that house with his own hands. He wanted it to stay in the family. So do Aunt Ida Mae and Otha and Cassandra. Only people acting like they don't understand is you and Debra Kay."

Well, on top of the fact that he was out of his mind if he thought I was going to take wise counsel from the likes of him, I didn't appreciate the disrespectful tone in his voice. *The nerve!*

"I don't want to make this a long legal process, Momma."

"I'm sure you *don't* wanna drag this out with the courts, 'cause me and you both know whose pockets gonna run dry first."

I heard Son shift the phone.

Now, I know what I said was a little nasty, but it was the truth.

While Son was stunned into silence by me bringing him back to reality, I jumped right in and tried to reason with him. "Look, Son, I know you are serious about wanting to keep the house in the family. I'm not saying I don't want that, too. But y'all not gonna bully me and Frank into making a hasty decision. And I don't know what kind of two-bit lawyer you got who still thinks sending something certified in a big envelope is enough to make somebody scared. That's the oldest trick in the book. He gonna have to come stronger than that if he intendin' to pry the keys to the house from *my* hand. Where you find him at... the barber shop?"

That's enough.

Well, I had a lot more I wanted to say, but I had to listen to the Spirit before I said some things I would have to take back.

Round about that moment, I heard the mumbling in the background. Men's voices calling my son's name. "Albert. Dude? *Albert.*"

I said, "Son, you there?"

"Albert!"

I heard people shuffling.

"Hello!" I yelled. "Anybody hear me?"

Someone said, "Call 9-1-1."

A lump hardened in my throat.

The line went dead.

Oh Lord! Jesus! I redialed the office number. It went straight to voicemail. Then I called again and pressed zero for his secretary.

She picked up and answered in a panicked tone, "Stonebridge Consulting, this is Stephanie. How can I help you?"

"This is Albert Jackson's mother. I was just on the phone with him. What's going on?"

"I'm not sure, ma'am. He's not responding at the moment. We have called an ambulance.

What, Lord? An ambulance? My mind instantly shifted gears. Son's my firstborn and—*ooh!*—I don't know what I'd do without that boy to worry me.

My entire body felt like a huge rock had smashed on top of me. I wondered what all Son had heard me say. Was his last words from me nasty and cutting? Or did he hear my softer words afterwards?

"Ma'am, are you there?" the secretary asked.

"Yes, I'm here."

"Some of the guys are trying to check for...vitals." Her voice broke with panicked emotion. "I...I don't know what else to tell you."

Poor child must have been terrified at what I was trying not to imagine.

"Okay. Thank you. I'll get hold of his wife."

My first phone calls was to my praying friends, Libby and Ophelia. I told them what I knew, and they was on it right away. I needed to notify Wanda, but if the truth be told, when every second counts, getting the Lord involved is more important than contacting next of kin.

Right after, I called Wanda and tried to present the news to her as calmly as possible. She started crying immediately. "Is he alive, Mama B?"

"I'm assuming he is. Go ahead and call up to his job and find out where they takin' him so you can meet them at the hospital. And let me know as soon as you hear something."

She assured me she would, but I know how your mind does in times like these. I needed to get back to my room and let my husband know what was going on, so we could pray and he could get to reaching out to his long-time doctor friends at the hospitals and maybe find out what was happening with Son. I know they got laws against that kind of stuff now, but Frank and the ones he been practicing with got ways around it, I understand. They look out for one another.

Soon as I walked into the room and saw Frank standing in the kitchen area fixing coffee, seem like a bunch of emotions flooded over me. Fear. Guilt. Regret.

He abandoned the coffee pot. "Now, B, I already told you not to let Son get to—"

"Something's happened to him." I crumbled in Frank's arms. "He passed out while we were talking on the phone."

"Baby, let's pray."

I know one thing, it's nice to have a grounded man around when your emotions threaten to wreak havoc all over the place.

17

I heard back from Wanda about an hour later. She said the doctors were pretty sure Son had suffered a major heart attack. "It's touch and go right now," she whispered over machines beeping.

"Wanda, we're all praying, honey. Don't get weary. Son's gonna need you to help him when this is all over."

"I'm so sorry," she squealed softly. "This is my fault."

"How you come to that conclusion?" Shoot, I had been blaming myself up until then. How did she figure she was gonna take this one on herself?

"Because I put a lot of pressure on him to make more money, to buy me more things, to keep up with my sisters. He told me he hated this job. He wanted to take an offer closer to home with less stress, but it would have paid a little less. I told him no because our cards are maxed and our credit isn't the best right now. Ever since then, he has been working like crazy. He put on twenty pounds in the last two months. And he started with all the symptoms of high blood pressure. Acting erratic, unreasonable—but I missed them. Too busy complaining. I told him if he didn't quit acting crazy, I was kicking him out. He didn't have anywhere to go. That's why he wanted to keep the house so badly. He wanted a place to live."

My Lord. This son of mine! Why couldn't he just tell me the truth? I already knew the answer to my own question. This was, after all, the son of Albert Jackson, Sr.

I could see right then and there the enemy was trying to make everything worse by divvying up blame amongst the family. I, for one, was out. And I was hoping to get my daughter-in-law to quit playing, too.

"Wanda, honey, don't you take on guilt right now. Son is a full grown man. He's the man of the house and he made his own choices. Besides all that, they call high blood pressure the silent killer for a reason. Usually ain't no symptoms, so people need to keep regular doctor appointments, which I'm sure Son wasn't doing. So don't go puttin' blame where it ain't due. I'm sorry it came to this, but I know God's gonna work it out."

"I don't know. They've got all these tubes in him, and..."

"Shhhh," I quieted her. "Don't let Son hear you speaking those words."

Let alone the enemy.

"How soon can you get here, Mama B?"

"I don't rightly know. Frank is on the computer downstairs checking the schedules."

Wanda sighed. "I wish you were here."

"Well, you got Somebody better. God. Talk to Him, you hear?"

She sniffed. "Yes. I will."

"I will be home as soon as I can."

FRANK CAME BACK from the business office and said there wasn't a plane with two empty seats until the evening, around 6. The tickets were gonna cost an arm and a leg, but Frank said it didn't matter. For once on this trip, we was on the same page.

"You might as well come on to the wedding, so we won't have to go back to the hotel for our things afterward," he suggested. "We can catch a cab to the airport after the reception."

I didn't have the strength or the mind to argue with him that morning. He got me to agree to go to breakfast and attempt to attend the wedding.

"You need to eat something, B. You need your strength."

"Okay."

As we sat at the morning buffet, I tore into my chicken sausage savagely. I wasn't thinking about no manners, wasn't thinking about no Kennedy and Gary. My time would be better spent in solitude, praying. That was my peace.

"I told Gary we'd be leaving early because of Son," Frank said. "He understands."

Whether he understood or not wasn't my concern, but I knew Frank was only trying to keep everything smooth. "That's good."

A few hours later, I was boarding a ferry to attend the wedding. The boat was at capacity, with 15 passengers, including the minister, bride, groom, me, Frank, Chad, the twins, the wedding coordinator, and six more from Gary's family, including his father who looked just like him.

Whether Kennedy was ignoring me or too nervous to look my way, I didn't care. Had more important matters swimming in my head. It was a constant battle to cast down fear for Son's sake.

For the sake of my husband, I pushed away my initial prejudice about the wedding altogether and focused on the fact that two people were about to enter a covenant that mirrored Christ's love for the church. Even if they were marrying for convenience, even if they were marrying so Gary could have a trophy wife, somewhere deep down inside both of them had some level of respect for holy matrimony. These days, folk live together indefinitely. Gary and Kennedy was goin' against the grain by making a formal commitment to one another. I chose to respect the day on that fact alone.

Kennedy sat in a lonely corner of the boat wearing a forlorn look. She sat fiddling with her mother's necklace.

I sat humming and groaning to the Lord under my breath.

When the boat's operator asked if that was every-one, Gary eyed Kennedy.

She shrugged. "I guess so."

Just as the operator was getting ready to untie the boat from the post, Whitney came running across the pier waving frantically. "Wait! Wait!"

Kennedy turned to see her sister. I don't know if anybody else noticed the smile in Kennedy's eyes except me, but there it was clear as day.

Until one of the twins made a low growl.

Kennedy must have suddenly remembered that she was supposed to be acting some kind of way toward her sister, to save face with her friends. Kennedy rolled her eyes. "Let her on."

Ooh, I coulda took that spring bouquet and bopped Kennedy upside the head with it. *Girl, this is your one and only sister!* She just don't know what some of us would do to see our sisters one more time. And given the fact that my child was in a hospital bed fighting for his life, the last thing I wanted to see was two family members at odds unnecessarily. Life's too short and could come to a screeching halt at any moment.

Whitney came and sat next to me and Frank.

"Glad you came," I whispered to her.

"Me, too."

Halfway to the little island, the rocking of the boat started getting to me. I ain't never been one to get carsick or seasick, but it got to me that morning. I quietly asked Frank how much longer we'd be on the boat.

"Gauging by how far we've been and how far away it looks, I guess another ten minutes. You okay?"

"Not really, but I think I can make it. I shouldn't have had such a large breakfast."

Whitney grabbed my arm. "I think I'm gonna be sick."

Her face might as well have been a green crayon, poor thang.

"Let's go to the other side of the boat."

Frank nodded in agreement.

I pulled Whitney to a standing position and we started making our way to the back, behind the center case and out of sight. We barely made it to the edge before Whitney leaned over the railing and her food came back up. Didn't take long for her stomach to empty, but she kept on heaving so loud afterward a few of Gary's family and even Frank came to check on her.

"She will be fine," I told them. You all can go back around."

Frank went and got Whitney a bottled water from the operator.

After a few sips, she was fine. Her normal color returned and the sweat beads disappeared from her forehead.

"You feel better?"

"Yes. Thank you."

"Atta girl."

I thought all would be fine after, but when we returned to the front area and most of the group started clapping for Whitney, all manner of craziness broke out.

"Would it kill you to let me have my wedding day to myself?" Kennedy screamed. "It's always about you, Whitney!"

Whitney grabbed her stomach. "It's called motion sickness, Kennedy. Google it."

Chile, I don't even know how to explain it to you, but next thing I knew, Kennedy had done put her sister in a headlock. Then they both fell to the deck and started rolling around.

Gary and Frank was trying to break them up.

The twins was half-screaming and half-laughing.

Chad got pushed to the side and his camera went flying into the water. He dove into the water to retrieve it. The operator hollered at him to get his skinny behind back on the boat. "These waters are not safe!"

The operator was also hollering at the girls to quit this fighting before they flipped the boat over.

At this news, everybody jumped in to pull those two apart.

"You two stop it!" I finally yelled like a mother fussing at two kids arguing over the front seat.

Somehow, they both heard and obeyed. Kennedy jerked away from Whitney. Stopped in their tracks on their hands and knees on the deck. Both of them breathin' like two pit bulls that just got pulled away from each other.

The operator pulled a gasping Chad and his camera back in the boat.

We all sat, stood, or kneeled, frozen in place as though we was doing one of them camera phone freeze challenges.

Then Whitney's eyes got real big as she stared at her sister's neck. "Mom's necklace!"

Kennedy touched her bare neck. "Oh my gosh!"

And all of a sudden the two of them started crying as they scrambled to retrieve the tiny beads that must have broken in the chaos and were scattering all over the deck, even rolling off the edge, as a result of their tiff.

The tiny countless multi-colored beads and shells were almost imperceptible from a standing position. But when I bent down to help, I could see them everywhere. "Come on, everybody. Let's help," I instructed our party.

Frank and everybody else over the age of 50 had to maneuver past their knees, but we all got down to help, despite wearing our fine outfits. Even Chad started looking, as though mining for gold. He reached out into the water again, trying to catch some of the beads that had rolled off the deck and were floating on the surface.

Lord, help us.

Only people who wasn't down helping was the twins.

"I'm so sorry." Whitney began to cry.

"You should be. It's all we have left of Mom," Kennedy wailed.

"I said I'm sorry," Whitney moaned again. She grabbed Kennedy's shoulder and made her sister pay attention. "I'm sorry for everything. You did everything for me and Mom. And I'm glad she gave you this necklace. You deserve it. You deserve all the happiness in the world."

Whitney took Kennedy's hand and poured the beads she had found into her older sister's cupped hands. The two embraced, crying and heaving painful sobs. Leaning on one another as they should have done a long time ago. But it's never too late to start.

One by one, we all approached those two, sitting on the deck knee-to-knee, and gave Kennedy what we had been able to recover of the broken necklace. The operator had even managed to pick up a few pieces, though I doubted he understood how precious each piece was to Kennedy and Whitney.

Whitney glanced at the beads in her sister's hands. "There were more. A lot more. I'm so sorry."

"It's not your fault. I started the fight," Kennedy admitted. "And now we've lost Mom again because of me."

I got down there with them before the enemy could wedge his ole' ugly head in. "Now, I know you lost some of the beads. But you got a whole lot more left than what you lost. You gotta stop focusin' on what's gone and focus on what's here. So what y'all gonna do with all these beautiful beads?

Kennedy held Whitney's hand close. "She was your mom, too." She gave some of the beads back to her sister. "Maybe instead of one necklace, we could make two bracelets?"

Whitney smiled. "Yeah. Two matching bracelets."

Them two hugged and my eyes watered at the sight. If their mother could see them now, she'd have been smiling from ear to ear. Her girls, finally moving on toward some peace after so many years of turmoil and strife between them.

A cough came from one of the twins. It was one of them fake coughs, and I knew it because the other twin smiled.

"Really?" Chad said. "Really? You think it's trash? Why don't you say it to their faces?"

Hot dog! My boy, Chad!

I guess I wasn't the only one who'd had enough of the two-faced wonder-river twins.

"No one said anything about trash," the leader said.

"Yeah, you did. I heard you," Gary seconded.

Uh oh! We got another witness!

"Same here," the coordinator said.

Kennedy and Whitney finally stood.

Kennedy looked around at the boat's inhabitants, then looked at her friends. "Your knees. They're dry and clean. Not like everyone else's."

The follower said, "Ummm...hello...we're wearing Juicy Couture."

Whitney pointed at Gary's aunt. "What are you wearing?"

"Donna Karan."

"And you?" she asked me.

To which I proudly replied, "I don't know, but it wasn't cheap."

"Seriously?" the twins said simultaneously.

"Yeah. Seriously," Kennedy repeated. "She was telling the truth about you two the other night. I kind of knew it. I didn't want it to be true, but obviously it is. I see now who my real friends are, and they're not you two. Don't come to my wedding. Take another ferry back."

"Are you kidding me? I'm your maid of honor," the bossy one protested.

Kennedy linked arms with her sister. "Not anymore."

FOR AS MUCH as I hemmed and hawed about Gary marrying somebody young enough to be his daughter, I was the main one sitting on the front row crying tears of joy like she was my own child. I wasn't a fan of the age difference, but I could see Kennedy was gonna be all right. She still had a lot to learn about herself. Still had to come into her own. But it was gonna be a whole lot easier without her playing a fake role.

And Gary wasn't a monster. His new bride was nearly thirty, after all. I just hoped and prayed that he was ready for this change to come in his wife. And his sister-in-law. I got the feeling that once Kennedy started exploring her own gifts and dreams, Gary might get more than he bargained for.

18

Debra Kay called just before we boarded the plane back to Dallas and said they were taking Son to surgery to repair a blockage. I held onto Frank's hand and prayed as we took off, asking the Lord to guide the surgeon's hands and strengthen my child's body to make it through the surgery and beyond. Son's problems was still gonna be there after the anesthesia wore off. It was high time he learned to turn every little part of his life over to the Lord. Can't nobody make it through this life in good health stressin' about this and that and trying to keep up with the Joneses.

Because I had taken some of that Dramamine to settle my stomach before the flight, I drifted off to sleep in my seat. And I had a dream. It was a replay of

Kennedy and Whitney on their hands and knees trying to catch those beads, crying and whimpering, scraping their knuckles against the deck in the attempt to salvage what they could of the memory of their mother.

Then all of a sudden, it wasn't Kennedy and Whitney no more. It was Son down there squirming and stretching, hollering, trying to get the beads. It was one thing to see two young girls down on the deck, but another to see a grown man in that same desperate position. I reached out to help Son. That's when I woke up because Frank was pulling my hand down in real life.

Frank squeezed my hand. "B, you were dreaming. You all right?"

"Yes," I said. "The Lord just showed me in a dream how Son feels just the same as those girls trying to hold on to what they could of their mother. I was trying to help Son just like I helped Kennedy and Whitney."

"Mmm."

I sat up and faced my husband. "Frank, I know you just looking out for my well-being by wanting to sell the house and make our future even more secure financial-wise, but I won't have no peace about taking it from my kids. I'm gonna give them the house when the time is right."

Frank conceded with a nod. "You think Son will keep the house up? Pay the taxes and such?"

"That ain't my problem. I want to leave this earth knowing I did everything in my power to set them up for success. I do believe that's what Albert, Sr. would have wanted. You can give your house to your kids when you go; it don't really matter to me. I can move to one of them senior places like Libby and have somebody cook my meals three times a day. The Lord been providing for me all this time, I believe He will continue the same."

"So that's your final word? You gonna make this decision without me?"

I wanted to tell him I was making that decision all on my own just like he made the decision to start a business without running it by me, but I wasn't gonna bring that up no more. The Lord was gonna handle that stuff, too.

Instead, I said, "I hope you will respect my choice, Frank."

He kissed my cheek. "I gotcha back, B."

Son made it through the surgery. The doctor said it was a miracle Son hadn't succumbed to a heart attack five years earlier, the way his valves was all cluttered up. Said Son could have died instantly that morning. "He's a lucky man."

Hmph. Luck ain't had nothing to do with it. The Lord knew my heart couldn't take it if Son and me was on bad terms when he left this earth. Shoot, even on good terms I'd be a mess if any one of my children passed on before me.

Wanda wanted to ask the doctor some more questions, so they stepped into the hallway. A few seconds later, she asked Frank to join their conversation to make sure she understood what was being said. My poor daughter-in-law's eyes was bloodshot and all her makeup smeared off from crying and hours of frazzlement. She definitely needed somebody to help her understand what the surgeon was saying in that moment.

I waited in the room with Son. He was in and out of consciousness, but he knew who we were and what had happened to him. I sat in the chair next to his bed, just rubbing the portion of his right arm that didn't have a tube in it. Humming and praying. Talking to the Lord in one breath and Son in the next, though he wasn't responding.

Not at first.

"Through it all, through it all," I sang, "I've learned to trust—"

"Momma." Son whispered, trying to remove the oxygen mask with his left hand.

I swatted his arm away. "Unh unh. Leave it on, Son. You all right."

He didn't have the energy to try again. "Momma. I'm sorry. About the house."

I stood up and kissed Son's forehead. "I'm sorry, too. But it's gonna be all right. Don't you worry about none of that. God showed me some things. Where I was wrong, too. We got to work together, Son, that's all. You and Wanda got to do the same, too."

I rubbed my head across Son's thinning hair. He had the same cowlick balding pattern as his daddy. Albert Sr. held on to that hair longer than he should have, if you ask me. He was sixty-one before he gave up the fight and shaved off the last few scraggly tufts. Stubborn thing, he was.

Since Son couldn't go nowhere or talk back, I took the liberty of giving him some unsolicited motherly advice. "Now, looka here. You gotta start taking care of yourself better. Going to your checkups and taking your medicine. And stop eatin' all that fast food, and get your behind back in church so you can get some sewn in your heart. You hear me, Son?"

"Unh hunh," he barely answered, drifting back off to sleep.

I heard Libby's voice from the other side of the door, talking to Wanda and Frank. She came on in, hugged me, and pulled the blessed oil from her purse, like me and her had already rehearsed this a million times. We prayed and anointed Son, then we quietly praised the Lord. Frank and Wanda came in a little later, and we all continued in soft prayer and praise.

Son lay there motionless and silent. But somehow I knew he could hear us deep down in his soul.

EPILOGUE

Thank God, Son quit that job. The other position, the one he had turned down, was still open. Wanda talked him into humbly contacting that employer and seeing if he could reactivate his application. Thank God, they said "yes." Son started the new job a few weeks after he was released from the hospital. I can't say that Son complained any less about work, but I could tell he was just complaining out of habit at that point - not because he was truly stressed.

Some people gonna complain whether sunshine or rain. I accepted that about my first husband and my firstborn. Wasn't no need in me getting all bent out of shape every time. A little grace goes a long way.

Son had to humble himself again and accept three appointments with a financial planner. Frank had a good friend who had helped him and his first wife through some tough times. They was real close to filing bankruptcy at one point, but this man had helped them get things in order before they got to that step.

Anyhow, Frank had a one-on-one, man-to-man meeting with Son. Told him that he had walked in Son's shoes. He knew what it was like to bear the responsibility of a being the man of the house. I gather they also talked a little about being a husband to a strong woman. Well, I don't know what all they discussed—Frank didn't tell me everything. I didn't expect him to.

The result of that meeting was Son agreed to meet with the financial planner. Next thing I heard from Son, he and Wanda had a strategy in place. They would be ready to fully take over the house year after next. In the meantime, me and Frank contracted with one of them property management companies to take some of the stress off ourselves.

As for Frank and Gary's business venture. *Ha!* Let me tell you what happened. Kennedy gave new life to those beads from the necklace and designed those bracelets for her and Whitney. Apparently everywhere she went, people was giving her compliments left and right. So she and Whitney started making these "sisterhood" bracelets and selling them online. You know Whitney already had a knack for drawing attention to herself. The Lord used her talent to help them get some marketing, and them bracelets took off like wildfire! I think folks was more touched by the story of how their first bracelets were made from their deceased mother's necklace than anything. It truly made for a feel-good story on the news shows and on their website.

Well, anyhow, Gary had to hold off on starting his business because he was too busy helping his wife with the bracelets. "We've got a huge deal on our hands right now with two major chains," he told me and Frank over the speakerphone phone one morning as we sat for breakfast.

Frank gave a genuine laugh. "You don't say?"

"Man, it's crazy." Gary laughed. "I might have to take off some time at the hospital until we get our production in place with supplies and workers. Running this is a lot more than I imagined, but I wouldn't have it any other way. I've never seen Kennedy so happy."

Frank threw one of them I-told-you-so smiles at me.

I should have been the one giving him the look 'cause Gary was saying everything I had been done told Frank—that running a business was just like having a newborn baby. Constant attention needed!

All I did was lean up and over Frank's phone and say, "Tell Whitney and Kennedy I said congratulations. I'm praying for their continued success. I am *well* aware running a business is gruelin'."

Frank swatted at my backside. I slapped at his hand.

"We appreciate the prayers," Gary said. "Kennedy created a style named after you. The Mama B. Beautiful brown beads, gold accents and shells. I've been meaning to give it to you, but I've been so busy between the hospital and the business."

I heard Kennedy fussing in the background, "You haven't given it to her yet?"

"No, honey, I—"

"Mama B," Kennedy's voice came through, "I am so sorry you don't have the bracelet yet. Whitney and I can bring it to you today. We wouldn't have this business if it weren't for you. Are you free for lunch?"

"I surely am."

"Okay. I'll text you a place and time."

"Looking forward to it, love."

Gary and Frank had a few more words before they ended the call.

Frank sat there, just staring at me. He clicked his cheek. "Guess you saw this coming, hunh?"

I sipped my tea, then innocently replied, "Honey, I took it to the Lord and left it there."

"I really thought the Lord was pushing me to help seniors. I don't like to see them taken advantage of."

"He very well may be calling you to take a stand,

Frank, but it's plenty of ways to help. You could volunteer. You could get involved in advocacy. You could teach classes at the church to seniors and their loved ones. God has a plan for this passion He put in you."

"Hmph." He patted my arm. Took a drink of his cranberry juice. "When you see Kennedy and Whitney today, I want you to get me one of them Mama B bracelets. Maybe if I wear it, it'll remind me to include you in my decisions."

"If that be the case, they gonna have to make a Frank bracelet, too, 'cause I need to be reminded sometimes, myself. I ain't perfect, you know."

"You sure getting mighty close, B. And you bringing me along, too."

"That's God bringing us both closer to Him, Frank. Sure is sweet, ain't it?"

"Sure is."

DISCUSSION QUESTIONS

1. Mama B says that although Son was 50-something years old in human-years, he was acting like he was fifteen in spirit-years. Do you think it's possible to have a huge gap between age and spiritual maturity? If you had to put an age on yourself to describe your spiritual maturity, how old would you be?
2. Mama B was disturbed by the age difference between Dr. Westhouse and Kennedy. At what point, if ever, do you raise your eyebrow concerning other people's relationships?
3. When Frank says that he believes Mama B is like Jesus, Mama B says she suspects that

the Holy Spirit communicates thoughts between Christian spouses. Do you think this is true? Does a marriage between believers differ from a marriage that is unequally yoked?

4. Son calls Mama B while she's on vacation. Frank intercepted the call and told Son to handle the business with the house and reminded Son that they were on vacation. Do you think Frank was out of line or do you think he was right to help Mama B draw a boundary?

5. Mama B says that marriage has taught her the difference between something that is "a sin unto God versus an annoyance unto me." Do you have a relationship that teaches you to accept differences? What have you learned about yourself in that process?

6. Before Mama B yields to God's will for her at the wedding, she says, "It ain't no sense in somebody prayin' and askin' God to get involved if they already done made up their mind to do whatever they want to do anyhow." Do you agree with her reasoning? Why or why not?

7. Frank wants to settle things based on the facts, but Mama B says he needs to take

people's feelings into consideration. How do you balance decisions? Do you lean more toward considering facts or feelings?

8. Kennedy says Whitney is a pathological liar. How do you deal with liars in your life?

9. Mama B recalls a time when she and a co-worker often interpreted the same event differently. How do you handle differences in relationships? Are you quick to become defensive or can you quickly agree to disagree?

10. Mama B realizes that she needs to stay prayerful even while she is on vacation because the enemy doesn't take breaks. Are there times when you are more apt to skip prayer time—weekends? Vacations? Busy seasons? Does this have an effect on your life?

11. What did you think of her analogy about prayer being as essential as brushing your teeth?

12. Frank says people have married for far worse reasons than stability and companionship. Would you agree? Do you think the desire for stability or companionship is an ill motive for marriage or not?

13. Mama B doesn't believe in drinking, but Frank has no problem with a glass of wine. Both are Christians. Is it possible for two believers to both be "right" and yet disagree?

14. Mama B says she knew in her knower that she didn't need to say anything else to Frank about his business idea. All she needed to do was keep quiet and let the Lord handle it. Have you ever had an instance where something you were concerned about worked out perfectly without you even getting involved?

15. Mama B says she wants to shoot Frank's idea down without shooting him down. How can you give critique in a way that preserves the other person's dignity?

16. When Mama B is talking to Whitney about her behavior on the cruise, she quickly switches from being critical to encouraging Whitney. What's more effective with you – criticism or encouragement? Why?

17. Mama B tells Whitney that her humility puts her at an advantage with God. What does God have to say about humility? Why do you think He adores humility?

18. Mama B says some people complain whether there's sunshine or rain. She has

accepted this trait in her loved ones. Do you find it easy to overlook others' faults or do you take them to heart? What faults do your closest friends and loved ones overlook in you?

PLEASE, PRETTY PLEASE LEAVE A REVIEW!

That's right. I'm begging (LOL)! In case you didn't know, good reviews help boost authors' visibility on in online stores. By writing a review, you help other readers make informed decisions about where to find the best information and entertainment. If this book was a blessing to you, please take a moment to share your experience at your favorite online book retailer.

And don't forget to join my email list! Be blessed!

MORE BOOK BY MICHELLE STIMPSON

No Weapon Formed – Revisit LaShondra and Stelson ten years after their whirlwind romance. Now married and the parents of two bi-racial children, they must learn to toggle faith and clashing cultures.

The Blended Blessings Series –Angelia didn't get it right with her first marriage. Or her second. She hopes this third time will work out, but with twin step-daughters and a mother-in-law who don't like the status quo, this may be the most difficult marriage yet.

A Forgotten Love – One bad play brought London Whitfield's brief professional football career to a devastating end. Back at home and reluctantly living life as an average Joe, London reconnects with the one girl, Daphne, who represents the best and the worst relationship he ever experienced.

All This Love - Knox Stoneworth got dumped at the altar—literally—and has spent the last few years burying himself in work to move past the pain. After a night of celebrating his parents' anniversary, Knox meets a stranger who just might change his mind about his future.

Married for Five Minutes - Take a 5-minute peek inside real marriages facing challenges that threaten to blur the reflection of Christ that marriage was created to be.

**Michelle has written more than 40 fiction and non-fiction books,
so be sure to check out her author pages at online retail stores!**

ABOUT THE AUTHOR

Michelle Stimpson's works include the highly acclaimed *Boaz Brown*, *Divas of Damascus Road* (National Bestseller), and *Falling Into Grace,* which has been optioned for a movie. She has published several short stories for high school students through her educational publishing company at WeGotta-Read.com.

Michelle serves in women's ministry and regularly speaks at conferences, events and writing workshops sponsored by churches, schools, book clubs, and educational organizations.

The Stimpsons are proud parents of two young adults, grandparents of one super-sweet granddaughter, and the owners of one Cocker Spaniel, Mimi, who loves to watch televangelists.

www.MichelleStimpson.com

VISIT MICHELLE ONLINE:

WWW.MICHELLESTIMPSON.COM

https://www.facebook.com/MichelleStimpsonWrites

CPSIA information can be obtained
at www.ICGtesting.com
Printed in the USA
LVHW031609280319
612190LV00001B/25/P